T0196073

IMMORTAL SOULS

John P. Smith

iUniverse, Inc.
New York   Bloomington

This is a work of fiction. All of the characters, names, incidents,
organizations, and dialogue in this novel are either the products of the
author's imagination or are used fictitiously.

iUniverse books may be ordered through booksellers or by contacting:

iUniverse
1663 Liberty Drive
Bloomington, IN 47403
www.iuniverse.com
1-800-Authors (1-800-288-4677)

Because of the dynamic nature of the Internet, any Web addresses or
links contained in this book may have changed since publication and
may no longer be valid. The views expressed in this work are solely those
of the author and do not necessarily reflect the views of the publisher,
and the publisher hereby disclaims any responsibility for them.

ISBN: 978-1-4401-5806-3 (sc)
ISBN: 978-1-4401-5807-0 (ebook)

Printed in the United States of America
Library of Congress Control Number: 2009934067
iUniverse rev. date: 8/03/09

Book One.

Pretty Emmylou Vessel of Souls

CHAPTER ONE

Olton Broads Boat Yard Summer of 1999.

The fleeing, descending, nymph was lost. She was searching, darting, and diving, first this way and then that. Time was running out. She and she alone knew who she was, or what she was. Or from whence she came. She had to find somewhere to take refuge, the dark was good. Yes, and so was the wood. The wood and the dark, she could almost hide away forever. Below her the river was cold and dark, it also lacked the shelter, she so craved, and the sanctuary she so badly needed. Boats were now appearing moored along the sides of the river, straining at their mooring ropes. She now slowed her darting, her diving, she could find not one moored boat with an entrance. She had to keep on looking. Then she saw it, set back from the river bank in dry dock was the half built hull which would become, in twelve months time, the boat that would go by the name of 'Pretty Emmylou.'

In the years gone by, the Goddess had been regarded as very powerful, and very pretty, and one who carried great beauty. She wasted no time descending down into the wooden hull. Wood was good, for she could make her beauty blend in with the wood. Her long flowing golden hair would become the woods natural grains. Her eyes and mouth would be as one with the natural wood knots. Her naked sexy body with dark skin would blend in very well. The nymph was as always very well hidden by the wood. With the human's naked eye, she could make herself elude detection. She was also growing hungry, hungry for souls, human souls. Which is just what Jimmy Johnson would find out for himself the very next day?

"Jimmy, Jimmy, just how much longer are you going to be sitting on that toilet for? If you don't hurry up you will be late opening up the yard." Oh my God Jimmy thought to himself, why is that woman always telling me something I already know. That woman, he was referring to was Caroline, He had gone down on bended knee some ten years ago and popped the question. Caroline had said yes right away. It was also in the same month of June that Jimmy's father had retired from the boat yard, and handed it over to Jimmy on a plate. So Jimmy had inherited his fathers business and a young, pretty wife both in the same month. Today, today of all days Jimmy was thinking to himself. He had wanted to open up the yard early today. It was this Tuesday they had planned to fit the 3.5 diesel engine into the hull of 'pretty Emmylou.' He tried to cast his mind back, what could it have been that he had eaten, to give him diarrhea, the like of which, he had never had before. Now here he was, sitting, again on the toilet for about the seventh time today, and it was still just running out of him just like water.

It was Jimmy's father, Albert, who had commissioned the building of 'Pretty Emmylou'. Out of his boat yard Albert operated twenty boats for the holiday makers. All the boats were all fully booked up, all throughout the holiday season. "Another boat makes for more profit." Albert had told Jimmy, 'Pretty Emmylou' will start making us a profit from year one. Albert told Jimmy one day before he had retired. Jimmy decided this was it; this was the very last toilet visit here, at home. As he washed his hands for the eighth time that day, he just hoped he could make it to the yard, or rather the yard toilet in time.

As Jimmy drove up to the still locked yard gates, he was clenching his buttocks, tight, or at lease at tight he could, while sat in the brown leather driving seat of his year old BMW. Most of his yard crew were there already waiting for the key holder to appear and to let them in. "Morning boss" they all shouted, as he quickly opened his window and passed the gate key, through the open window to the nearest employee, who happened to be called Roger. Who looked pleased that Jimmy had chosen him to unlock the yards gates? Jimmy however was not pleased. He made a guess, if he didn't get to the toilet in about one minute flat; he would be going home again, to change his smelly clothes. It was more by luck than judgment; that Jimmy just made it to the toilet with ten seconds to spare.

When at last Jimmy first walked into his office his secretary was already busy on the phone. First he noted the strong aroma of; Jimmy was guessing a new perfume. Next he glanced at the open top four buttons, of her white, tight fitting blouse, which was trying hard to hide a nice white lace bra. But somehow her thirty nine inch 'D' bra looked too small for her large assets. Her blouse and bra also did nothing to hide her sexy cleavage. Jimmy was guessing she had doused that very same cleavage with her new perfume that very morning.

After replacing the hand set of the phone, and making some notes on the note pad, she looked up and smiled, at her boss. "Are you OK Jimmy? You look kind of pale." She told him. "I'm fine thank you Sandy, or I would be if I didn't have the shits." Jimmy told her. Sandy laughed, "Has that wife of yours been trying to poison you again?" She wanted to know. The office door was then opened from the outside. In the door way stood Roger. "Roger, for Gods sake, how many times do I need to you, if the office door is shut, then you knock, Ok?" "Yeah Sorry Boss I forgot. " "Who knows" Jimmy went on. "I may well have had Sandy bent over this here desk, with her tight green skirt, pulled up, her black sexy panties, pulled down and I, could have been in the middle of giving her a portion of, what women want." Jimmy looked at Sandy, her face was as red as a beetroot, come to that so was Rogers. "So what did you want Roger?" Jimmy asked. "We want you boss, we have everything organized, the engine, the crane, the fuel lines, everything." "Ok Roger give me ten minutes and I'll be there." Roger however did not move from the door way. "Was there anything else Roger?" Jimmy wanted to know. "Well yes, well no, boss, not really," replied Roger. "Come on Roger if you have something to say then say it." "It's that hull, the hull of 'Pretty Emmylou' its not the same, it's changed somehow."

"Roger, me and you built that hull how the hell could it change?" "When I was working on her just now, getting everything ready, ready to fit her engine, a strange feeling came over me." Sandy looked at Jimmy and winked. "Was it a sexual feeling?" Sandy asked of Roger. Sandy could tell she had hit a raw nerve. For the second time that day Roger's face was as red as a beetroot. "No shut up, she told me I was a too finer a man to still be a virgin." "Who, who told you that Roger." Asked His boss. "No just shut up about the whole thing, I'll go and wait for you at the hull, OK?" With that Roger turned and closed the office door behind him. Jimmy looked at Sandy, and Sandy looked at Jimmy. "If only I were still a virgin." said Sandy. "You and me both." Replied Jimmy.

Jimmy found Roger with a bizarre look on his face waiting for him, in the hull of 'Pretty Emmylou' everything is ready boss. Roger reported.

Three hours later the engine was fixed and fitted. Roger had gone out to a breakdown leaving Jimmy single-handedly working in the hull, fitting the propeller shaft and bearings. When a weird and wonderful feeling overcame him. First it was the feeling of being watched, followed by a warm almost sexual feeling. Jimmy looked around, he was sure he was still alone, but that feeling would not go away. Then he saw her, well her face anyway, it looked at first like a drawing, a picture, which maybe Roger had drawn, on the wood of the hull, while he had been waiting for Jimmy. The more Jimmy looked at it, the more it seemed to come to life. And the more beautiful the drawing became. Then Jimmy realized it was not a drawing, not a picture, because eyes in a picture did not blink, now did they? As

Jimmy watched, the wood below the face now seemed to distort also, and that distortion started to turn into a body of an appealing and beautiful woman. Jimmy could not take his eyes off this exposed body which was now walking towards him. "Who are you, where did you come from?" Jimmy asked. *"I am anyone who you want me to be, and I came from wherever you want me to come from."* Was her reply. Right before Jimmy's eyes, her image started to fade, until he could hardly see it at all. Then all of a sudden it returned, but not as the naked body he had seen before. Now the image was of Sandy, He had, had dreams about Sandy being undressed and here she was, wearing only her new perfume and now standing just five feet away. *"Well are you going to make love to me, or just look at me?"* Jimmy didn't need asking twice, he quickly unzipped his flies and pulled out his already erect eight inch weapon. Jimmy then held out both his arms inviting her to come closer. The very second before he was about to embrace her he was interrupted. "JIMMY, JIMMY, are you down there?" It was Sandy's voice calling him, Jimmy looked up and standing there looking down at him was the real Sandy. The Sandy, who he was just about to shag, had gone. "Jimmy it's the- she begun to say, Then, when she saw Jimmy standing in the hull with a eight inch erection protruding from his trousers, she quickly covered her eyes with her hands. "Jimmy I'm so sorry, I didn't mean too-" "No don't worry, I, I, don't know what came over me." Jimmy said while putting away his weapon. Still anxious not to uncover her eyes, Sandy said, it's the phone for you, you left your mobile in the office, that's why I came looking for you." "Well just tell whoever it is, I'm busy and will call them back, Ok." When Sandy turned and left, Jimmy had time to think about what had just happened. One minute an unclothed Sandy was standing in front of him wanting a shag, if in fact it had been Sandy, which of course it couldn't have been. Because the next minute, Sandy was looking at him fully clothed and in distress. Whatever must she think of him now, that's what Jimmy wanted to know? Then he remembered Roger said he had a funny feeling while in the hull. Jimmy wondered if Roger had seen a naked Sandy as well. Jimmy walked over to the part of the hull where he thought he had first seen the face appear, however apart from the grains in the wood, he could see nothing. If however Jimmy had touched the wood in that spot he would feel how warm it was. Warm in contrast to the coldness of the rest of the hull anyway.

Jimmy had been avoiding Sandy and the office, all day, just through utter and total embarrassment. When he could think of no excuse whatsoever, Jimmy decided he would come clean and tell her the truth. By now the day was coming to an end, and he could put it off no longer. Jimmy found Sandy sitting at her office desk, looking into her handbag mirror, putting on her face before she went home. "Sandy, I, don't know what, to, say-." Jimmy began, as always Sandy spoke her mind, always had done, and always would. That was one of the things about her, that her many friends liked so much. "Oh so Jimmy does not know what to say, is that right? Is this the same Jimmy who stood in a boats hull with an eight inch erection sticking out of his trousers in broad day light? Well let me tell you something JIMMY, you better think of something to say, and damn quick, and then I will decide whether or not I'm going to come to work tomorrow. Or whether or not I'm going to go to the police station." Jimmy could see he was not going to be able to joke his way out of this one. Jimmy held up his hands, his palms facing Sandy. He then sat himself down on a chair and rubbed his hands across his eyes, as if he was admitting defeat. "Well Jimmy I'm still as mad as hell, and I'm still waiting to hear just what it is you have to say." "Ok," Jimmy began, "But please don't interrupt me until I've finished, agreed?" "Ok Jimmy agreed." "Roger, remember Roger this morning? He said there was something wrong with that hull, he said something had changed, he said he had an odd feeling while alone in that hull. Well so did I, I had a strange feeling when I was all alone in that hull as well. I saw, I saw, well I'm not too sure who, or what I saw, at first, anyway. I can only describe her as an appealing naked gorgeous woman. I did ask her who she was, and from where she came. She said she was anyone I wanted her to be. Her image then faded somewhat, when the image came back, she had changed, she had changed into you. It was you, you were standing before me, in that hull, or at least I thought it was you. I only found out it was not you when you called me, and I looked up and saw you standing there." "Is that it Jimmy, have you done?" Jimmy nodded his head, he had given it his best shot everything now rested on Sandy's reply. Sandy started to shake her head slowly from side to side. "I don't know what to think Jimmy really I don't. For a start I can't believe that for one minute you would think of me standing naked in front of you in a boat's hull wanting you to make love to me. And specifically with that tiny eight inch dick, which is no good to anyone, even for stirring their tea with. However, on the other hand if you're not well you could have been suffering from illusions." "What about Roger then was he having illusions as well." Jimmy asked, Sandy. "I know what we can do," went on Jimmy "you wait here give me fifteen minutes, I'll go down in the hull alone, then you creep down to the hull as well and sneak a quick look inside and see if you see anyone else down their as well as me." "Jimmy just shut up will you, in a minute you will make me as crazy as you are." "Jimmy I don't know what to think, but what I do know is, I'm going home now to think about everything, I'll let you know what I've decided to do about it all tomorrow."

But what Sandy didn't know was, tomorrow was not going to come for Jimmy.

That evening after everyone had gone home, Jimmy himself could not understand just what had happened to him down in the hull of 'Pretty Emmylou' so before he himself went home as well, he decided to pay just one more visit to the hull. The light was starting to fade, as Jimmy walked around in the hull, he felt nothing, nothing at all. He began to think he was on a fool's errand, when he felt it, someone or something was watching him. "Who's there?" Jimmy called out. Silence, no reply at all. He turned around, and there she was, standing there, he saw Sandy, it had to be Sandy. She was wearing the same clothes, the same perfume as she had been wearing all day. "Sandy I thought you had gone home." Jimmy said. *"And just why would I do that Jimmy?"* She wanted to know. The Goddess was now slowly undoing the buttons of her white blouse. Jimmy of course could not tear his eyes away. *"We are going to play a little game Jimmy. I want you to take off your belt, and put it around your neck, that's right, do it up nice and tight. You are being a good boy for me tonight Jimmy aren't you? Now tie the other end of your belt to the hook of the crane."* Then, without further ado the crane whirled into life. All too late Jimmy realized just what was happening, the crane had now lifted him off his feet, and with both hands he grabbed the belt trying to free himself from it. He tried to shout for help, but all he heard was a gurgle sound coming from his throat. His arms and legs were thrashing about, making every effort to try to get himself free. But it was a futile attempt, now the Goddess took hold of both of Jimmy's feet with her hands. *"Goodbye Jimmy"* she whispered, and with a good long hard pull, she heard the cracking of Jimmy's neck bones.

Caroline was wearing a worried look on her face. Jimmy was now a whole two hours late home. She had phoned the yard, and reached the answer machine. Jimmy's mobile just kept on ringing. Now clutching at straws, she had dialed Sandy's home number. Sandy answered it on the forth ring. "Hello Sandy, it's Caroline here, I'm so sorry to bother you at home." "It's no problem Caroline, what can I do for you?" "It's just that, well, It's just that Jimmy should have been home two hours ago, I just wondered if you had any idea where he might be." "Well no, sorry Caroline I don't, I left the yard at my normal time, and he was still there then, and as far as I knew he was going home himself." "I'm sorry Sandy I've tried phoning the yard and his mobile,

I didn't know who else to call." "Don't worry Caroline, you know Jimmy he just well have stopped off at the pub for a quick one." A quick what, that's what I would like to know, thought Sandy to herself. But she didn't say it out loud.

After Sandy had put down the phone, a bad feeling came over her. Her mind replayed to her the events of today. Roger and Jimmy talking about something wrong with the hull, about how it's changed somehow. And I'm sure Jimmy would never have gotten out his erection like that normally, now would he? Sandy sat down to watch TV, but she could not settle. She told herself she was being stupid, she now knew she would not sleep tonight unless she went back to the yard to make sure everything was alright.

When Sandy drove up to the yard gates, she was surprised to see them still standing open. She drove into the car park and was again surprised to see Jimmy's car still in the car park. She bent down and touched the tire on the offside front wheel. Stone cold, which told Sandy the car, had not been driven for a good while. She walked over to the office door, and found it locked. Using her key she unlocked it and went inside. "JIMMY" she called out as her right hand located the light switch. Light flooded the office, but still no sign of Jimmy. She sat at her desk and dialed Jimmy's home number. Caroline answered on the second ring. "Hello Caroline, it's Sandy, listen is Jimmy home yet?" "No he's not and now I'm as mad as hell, I've thrown, his dinner in the bloody bin-" "Caroline" interrupted Sandy, "listen to me, I'm at the yard now everything here is in order, Jimmy's car is still here but there is no sign of him at all." "Ok" began Caroline, "Sandy, do you mind waiting there for me, I'm going to come right on over."

It was twenty minutes later when Caroline pulled up next to Sandy's and Jimmy's cars. "So where have you looked already?" Caroline demanded, of Sandy as soon as she set eyes on her, Sandy had been waiting for her in the now dark car park of the yard. "Well so far in the office block, and workshop." Sandy began. "But what about down there? By the waters edge and the dry dock." Caroline went on," she then pointed in the general direction of the dirty water of the river, and the dry dock. "Not yet" began Sandy "it's dark down there now, without lights we won't see much." "Oh my God, then go get some Sandy, go and get a flash light or something, so we can go and have a look down there, by the river." Sandy turned around and headed towards the workshop where she was sure she would find some lights of some description. But Sandy didn't want to go and have a look down there, Sandy didn't want to go anywhere near the dry dock, anywhere near the hull it held there. "Maybe we should call the police." Sandy began as she returned with two flash lights. "Well Sandy I'm going down there to have a look, and I'm going to go down there now, with or without you." Caroline informed Sandy. "Ok, ok," said Sandy, "let's go then." First they walked along the waters edge, shining their bright flash lights, looking everywhere. Now they were coming up close to the dry dock, straight ahead of them. "Is there a boat in the dry dock, at the moment?" Asked Caroline, "That's where they are building the hull for the new boat," answered Sandy. Sandy's small inner voice was screaming at her, "Don't *look in there*

Sandy." By now Caroline had reached the hull and was shining her flash light all around, inside the hull, Sandy braced herself, fearing the worst. "That's strange" said Caroline, "what's that hanging from the hook of the crane?" Slowly Sandy shone her flash light down into the hull as well. She remembered perhaps just nine hours ago she had stood on this very spot, looking at Jimmy's eight inch erection. "I'm not sure" said Sandy "it looks like, a, I know what it is it's a belt, yes that's what it is it's a belt." "It's Jimmy's belt" said Caroline, "but why is it tied to that crane hook, and just where the hell is Jimmy?"

Jimmy could see and hear everything that was going on, if Caroline and Sandy had looked hard enough, and long enough at that part of the wooden hull, they would have seen Jimmy's face, or the face which had once belonged to Jimmy, now imbedded in the wooden hull.

Jimmy's body was never found Albert came out of retirement to take charge of the yard once again. The boat 'Pretty Emmylou' was finished about a year later. And a very impressive looking boat it was as well. The bright red wooden hull shone brightly in the sunlight. The wooden cabin and wheel house, was painted White. Yes if Jimmy could see it from the outside he would have been a proud man.

Two years after that Albert had to sell the yard due to his own ill health. Everyone at the yard got to keep there jobs, the new owners brought the whole yard as a going concern.

CHAPTER TWO

Two years later

The Robinson family were all in high spirits as they travelled in their two year old dark blue ford. The explanation for this was, they were going on holiday and for the very first time they were going cruising. It had given Victor quite a task persuading Margret, how much fun it would be to go cruising up and down the waterways of the Norfolk Boards. "It's left; the sign said Olton Broads to the left." Margret told Victor, her husband of nineteen years. Their two children, Mary, who was twelve, and John, who was two years older. Were, in the back of the car with the family pet Rex who was a four year old Yorkshire terrier. "Ok don't panic" Victor told Margret. "I'll turn around at the next roundabout." It was only after Margret had looked in the holiday brochure, and saw a picture of the boat that Victor had picked out, she had then read, that it had all been fitted out, with all the mod cons. Yes Margret did like her mod cons.

Not twenty odd miles away found Roger on this Saturday morning stressed out at the boat yard.

Saturday's had always been their busiest day of the week. Boats that had been hired out for the last week were being returned to the yard. Where any repairs had to be made, they all had to be refueled, the water tanks filled, and they all had to be cleaned, from top to bottom. All this had to be done ready for the holiday makers who had hired the boats for the following week. Even now after all this time, Roger still hated that boat, 'Pretty Emmylou', come to that so did everyone else who worked at the yard. Even the cleaning crews would never work on that boat alone. Everyone all said the same thing, everyone thought that the boat had to be haunted, or cursed, or something. After all they could not all be wrong.

The Robinson's dark blue Ford at last pulled into the boat yard car park. "John, make sure you put on Rex's lead, before you let him out the car" Victor reminded his ginger headed son. Who was by now nearly as tall as his father. While Victor and Margret went to reception to book in John and his younger sister Mary walked along the water's edge looking at all the boats, all moored up, ready and waiting for their next weeks crew's, to arrive. "John, Mary, have you seen a boat called 'Pretty Emmylou' yet?" called Margret, when at last she reappeared from the reception office, with Victor and a boat man who was called Roger. "Don't think so, not yet anyway," called back John. "It might be down here further. "Yes it is right on down there further" said Roger. The small group then walked along the water's edge until they came to a fine looking craft, with the name 'Pretty Emmylou' painted on the front of her bow, in white letters. "Here she is" said Roger, "all ship shape and ready and waiting for her new crew. Now everyone clime aboard and I'm going to show you around the craft and answer any questions that anyone might have." With that everyone made a move forward, well everyone except Rex that is. Rex just stood still moving his head first this way then that way, and sniffing all the time. John gave a sharp tug on his lead. All that achieved was to make Rex straighten his front legs and dig them in. He then bared his teeth and let out a low growl. John's Mother told John to just pick him and carry him aboard. Rex however was having none of it. First he darted this way and that way for as far as his lead would allow he was by far too fast for John to catch him. "It's that boat" said Victor; he is petrified of that boat." "Has he ever been on a boat before?" Asked roger. "Well no never" answered Margret. "What are we going to do?" "What we do" said Roger "is walk on till we come to the next boat and see if your dog is afraid of that one as well." The next boat they came to was called 'Dark Waters.' "Everyone come aboard" instructed Roger, everyone did, John bent down picked up Rex and without further commotion stepped aboard. Once aboard he bent down released Rex on the deck, who went off happily to have a good sniff around. "That's peculiar" began Victor, he does not like that boat, but the point is what are we going to do about it. Roger was not at all surprised Rex was terrified of 'Pretty Emmylou' hell, he and everyone else at the yard was as well. "The only thing I can do is to let you swap boats." Roger went on, "all our boats have everything, onboard just the same as 'Pretty Emmylou.' The only difference is they are not as new as 'Pretty Emmylou.'" Margret looked at Victor, Victor looked back at Margret. They were both thinking the same thing, how disappointed the kids would be if they had to cancel the holiday. Victor looked at Roger, "well that's very kind of you," said Victor; yes we would like to swap boats please." Which was good luck for the Robinson family, but not however for the Bean's who, would now be given the boat, which was meant for the Robinson's.

Betty Bean was not a happy woman, and because of this her husband Tony was not a happy man. The main reason Betty was not happy was because all her married life, all eighteen years of it, they had been trying for a child. Over the years they had both had all the tests, every Doctor could find nothing wrong with either of them. They had spent thousands of pounds nothing worked. Betty had decided she would give up trying to get pregnant, and just live out the rest of her life in anguish. They had now both been sitting in this old banger of a rusty old VW, for the last five hours. It was rusty because the green paint was twelve years old, and did no longer protect the metal underneath. After spending all that money trying to get pregnant this was the best car they could afford.

It was about an hour after the Robinson family had guided the cruiser, meant for the Bean's down stream that the Beans now arrived at the boat yard. Once again Mr. and Mrs. Bean were not happy. This was because they were now being told by a stressed out Roger that the boat they had hired was not now available. But it was their lucky day, due to the fact that he would upgrade the Bean's boat free of charge. This did put the smile back on Betty's lips.

Betty felt it the very moment she first set foot on the deck of 'Pretty Emmylou' it was a feeling, the kind of sexual feeling to send a tingle right down anyone's spine. As Betty and Tony were being shown around the boat, by Roger, Betty realized she was becoming more and more sexually aroused. She had the urge to keep tightly crossing her legs, every time she crossed them; she became more and more aroused. The last time Betty had felt like this must have been about eighteen years ago just before she was married.

Now three hour after they had picked up the boat from the yard, Tony was in the cockpit guiding 'Pretty Emmylou' down river, looking for a good place to moor up for the night. Betty was sunbathing on the bow deck. When, she at first heard the beautiful voice calling out in distress. Betty sat up hastily and shaded her eyes from the sun with her right hand. Suddenly she located where the shouting was coming from. Standing on the water's edge looking down and pointing into the river, was the prettiest woman Betty had ever seen. She had long flowing golden waist long hair, which was gently stirring in the breeze? At first, due to the drone of the powerful diesel engine, Betty could not understand just what it was the woman was shouting about. She jumped to her feet and shouted to Tony to cut the engine. Tony pulled back on the throttle lever, but as boats have no bakes the boat kept on going. Tony knew the way to stop a boat is to put the engine in reverse. Now with the engine cut, Betty could hear what it was the pretty long golden haired woman was shouting. *"HELP, PLEASE SOMEONE HELP, MY BABY IS IN THE RIVER, PLEASE I CAN'T SWIM,*

PLEASE SOMEONE SAVE MY BABY." Betty could hear the desperation in the poor woman's voice. She looked down in to the river to where the woman was pointing. Sure enough just under the water Betty could see the head and clothes of what currently looked like a baby. Betty could feel the pain and anguish of that poor woman. She shouted to Tony to stop the boat, Tony, had no idea what or who his wife had seen, he just knew she wanted him to stop the boat. So he put the engine into reverse, and pushed forward the throttle lever. The engine roared into life and started to bring the boat to a stand still. Betty hesitated not one moment longer. She was a strong swimmer and the baby was not that far away from the water's edge. Without having another thought, for her own safety, Betty dived off the boat and into the cold muddy water of the river. The Goddess knew this was a good part of the river, because here there was a very strong under current. By far too strong for the best of swimmers. The boat by now had nearly come to a standstill; Tony pulled back the throttle lever to the neutral position. Or rather he tried, to pull back the throttle lever to the neutral position. But it was impossible the lever was jammed, Tony could not shift it one inch. He watched Betty dive into the water; he watched her thashing about, to try to keep herself afloat, She was still struggling, when the under current slowly but indisputably sucked her down deep into the water, and underneath the boat. Tony saw two visions in his mind, the first vision was of Betty being sucked under the water, and dragged underneath the boat. The second vision is the vision Betty would have seen as she was pulled nearer and nearer, to the boats propeller, which was spinning around at a good speed of 3,000 rpm. It was a lucky thing for Tony that he did not see what happened next. Betty could see she was heading towards the boat's propeller. The currant was far too strong; Betty was powerless to save herself. She tried to grab the underneath of the hull with her hands but it was too smooth nothing for her fingers to get a grip onto. It was her hands that first came into contact with the spinning blades, the blades sliced off both of her hands like a knife through butter. At this point Betty felt no pain; she just saw her blood turn the muddy water red. Red with her own blood, that was now pumping out of her wrists. Her next body parts to hit the blades were her arms, just above her elbows, again the blades sliced off her arms with no difficulty. This time she did feel the pain. But she had no time to think about it, because the blades were still spinning, just missing her head by inches. The blades however did not miss Betty's neck, the neck that had been kissed so many times in moments of passion. Now the blades sliced through her neck cutting her head clean off. Again all the blood that still pumped out of her neck turned the water redder still. At that very moment when Betty's life ended, the throttle lever became free. Tony was now able to push it into the neutral position. He rushed to the port side of the boat and looked overboard into the water shouting Betty's name. Nothing. He then rushed to the stern of the boat, and again looked overboard. His first thought was, *why is the the water red?* Then he saw something floating in the water, it was hair, it was Betty's hair. Hair that was still attached to her head. And just to give him a better view of the head, it then turned it's self upside down. Letting the stem of Betty's neck protrude from the waters surface. Next about four feet away he saw Betty's hand, or at lease a hand that once belonged to Betty, also just bobbing about up and down in the water. Tony's mind then made the connection, The red water was blood, Betty's blood, the hair, still attached to her head, which was now unattached from her body, and not to mention the hand that was also unattached. The boats propeller belonging to 'Pretty Emmylou' had just murdered his wife Betty.

About seven hours later, things were not looking good for Tony. He was sitting on one side of a table in the Olton Boards police station making a statement. "So Mr. Bean," began Inspector Peter Rogers. "You have no idea why your wife should suddenly, jump up from where she was sunbathing, on the deck of the boat, and then diving into the river to her death? You see we have no witnesses, no one saw what happened. You also claim the throttle lever became jammed, we however had the boat checked over, by an independent marine engineer, who found no fault whatsoever with the throttle lever or linkage. Now do you see our predicament Mr. Bean?"

If, the so called independent marine engineer had looked very closely at the wooden hull, the thought would have crossed his mind that the builder who had built the hull must have been so bored, so much so that he had, had time to draw pictures of faces, onto the wood.

CHAPTER THREE

"Judy, phone," called out Mike, "who is it Mike? "I think it's the boat yard, someone called Roger Long returning your call." Mike and myself were two newspaper reporters, in fact the only two reporters who worked for the Olton Gazette. "Roger thank you so much for returning my call." I began, "my name is Judy Andrews, and I'm a reporter for the Olton Gazette. I'm covering the story of the tragic accident involving one of your boats." "Yeah so, what is it you want to know," Roger said coldly. "For a start why are you calling it an accident?" Roger went on. "It was no accident that the woman was sunbathing on the deck. Then for some unknown reason, just stood up, dived in the river, and got sucked underneath the boat. However if you were to ask me, is there something weird and wonderful about that boat, I would have to tell you the truth, and say. Yes there is something strange about that boat." "Roger" I said, "now I'm intrigued, go on tell me more." "I'm at work now and I can't talk here." he told me, "Then how about we meet up somewhere after work?" I suggested. "Yes fine" he said, "how about down by the river near the old windmill?" What I thought to myself, if this prick thinks I'm going to meet him on a dark night miles from nowhere, on my own, and down by the river. He can damn well think again. "Roger" I said, "no, I know, let's meet in the Fox and Hound pub, in the high street. And, I'm going to buy you a drink; do you know where it is?" Roger seemed to like this idea, "of course I know where it is. I'll be there about seven when I finish work."

"What was that all about?" asked Mike. "Just this jerk called Roger, works at the boat yard; he's got something to tell me about that boat. You know the one I'm doing this story about. I'm meeting him tonight." "Want me to come along?" Mike wanted to know. "No it's ok I'll be fine, why do you think I'm meeting him in a pub." On that very evening, at about 18:50 found me sitting on a bar stool at the bar with a Bloody Mary in front of me. It must have been years since I last had a Bloody Mary. I had forgotten the lovely warm feeling that followed the Vodka as it found it way down into my stomach. Apart from me, I could count everyone else in the bar on both hands. Also because I was the only woman, I was collecting masses of looks. Most of them aimed at my plentiful breasts. Of which I had always been proud of. I soon realized I was gathering too many, so I decided to button up my third button down from the top, of my work blouse. The barman also seemed to find a lot more to do up this end of the bar, than he did at the other end.

It was dead on the stroke of seven that Roger walked into the bar. After he made a quick glance around, saw that I was the only woman, he walked nervously over to me. "Err excuse me, I'm sorry, I, err, I'm, looking for Judy, Judy Andrews." I put him out of his misery. "Then look no further young man, because here I am, as large as life." I held out my right hand, expecting him to shake hands. But Roger had other idea's taking my right hand in his he turned my hand over, lifted it up to his mouth and kissed the back of it. Something a man would have done some hundred years ago. "I'm pleased to meet you Roger, thank you for coming." "No, no, no," began Roger thank you for coming." We both became aware of the barman hovering. "What can I get you to drink Roger?" I asked. "No, no, no, what can I get you to drink?" Two things told me Roger was now overcoming his shyness. One he was demanding to buy me a drink, and two his eyes started drifting down to my thirty seven inch bosom. "Well if you insist Roger, I'll have a Bloody Mary, thank you very much." We took our drinks over and found a corner table next to the juke box. I didn't want to start Roger off straight away talking about the boat. I wanted to loosen his tongue first with the whiskey and soda he was drinking. When we were about to start our third drink I was starting to feel my tongue was loose, never mind about Roger's. So without further ado I took my pen and pad out of my bag, and asked Roger, my first question. "So Roger, tell me in your own words, what do you think is wrong with that boat?" "Ah that's an easy question" began Roger. "It's haunted, that's all that's wrong with that boat it's haunted and that is all." "So when did you first think it was haunted, Roger?" "It was the day; I was down in the hull all alone." Roger now paused, "go on" I prompted. He did continue but not before his face turned as red as a beetroot. "Well I was in the hull, which was the day we were going to fit the engine, I was getting everything ready and I was waiting for Jimmy. All of a sudden I turned round and there she was." "There who was Roger?" "I don't know her name, I have never seen her before in my life, and I have never seen her since. She was so pretty, and she was stark naked, not wearing nothing she was. She had this long golden hair right down to her waist. Some of it was hiding her bear breasts but I could still see her rose bud red nipples, peeping throught her strands of long golden hair. While I was looking at her, she spoke, to me she said something like." *"Hello Roger, as you very well know you are a too finer man to still be a virgin, but don't worry I'm going to soon change all that."* "So what did you do then Roger?" Again he colored up, "I, I, got sort of scared, I turned and ran, I ran all the way to the office to find Jimmy." "Sorry, Roger who is Jimmy?" "Jimmy is my boss, sorry was my boss, a funny thing happened to him as well." "Ah yes I remember something about him, he owned the yard, well until he disappeared that is." "Yes he did, they found his belt, but that's all they found, no body or anything. And do you know where they found his belt? Tied to the crane hook inside the hull of 'Pretty Emmylou'. "So Roger do you think that boat is responsible for the disappearance of Jimmy, and the death of Mrs. Bean?" "I don't know Judy, I'm sorry I just don't know. But one thing I do know is, please never ever, go on that boat alone, never." I looked at my watch, and realized it was later than I thought it was. "So Roger can I quote you in my story, please?" "No, please don't do that, the new owners would not like me talking about one of their boats like this. "Ok Roger whatever you say. But what if I wanted to hire that boat for a week, how would I go about it?" "Just phone the boat yard, don't let them put you off, they are thinking twice about hiring out that boat, because every time they do something happens. And remember don't go aboard that boat alone."

It was well getting on for 23:00 when I at last arrived home. I was not expecting my husband Paul to still be up, however he was. "Hello babe," Paul began I've just started watching this film on cannel four, are you going to join me?" "No Paul I'm going to bed," I sat down on Paul's lap wrapped my right arm around his shoulders and kissed him, long and hard. In return his right hand found first my knee, and then started to caress the inside of my thigh. I opened my legs to allow his hand a clear means of access up to my waiting pussy. Which was becoming moist within the restrictions of my white lace panties. "Mmmm, oh Paul that feels so good, keep going, or shall we go upstairs?" However we only made it half way up the stairs, when Paul's hands went right up my shirt, he slipped his fingers inside the top of the waist band of my white damp lace panties. Then in one movement he slipped them all the way down my legs to my feet. "Paul I protested you're going to trip me up." "No I'm not, this is as far as we go, just bent over where we are." I did what I was told, and bent myself well over. Paul then slipped my panties off from my feet; next he parted my legs with his hands. "Paul what are you doing-" I began, as if in answer to my question, his head was now in between my legs. He was kissing every inch of my thighs starting just above my knees, and then slowly working his way up, higher, and higher, inch by inch. I giggled and wiggled, "Oh Paul don't tickle me, you make me want to pee, and I was not joking, I did need to pee." At last his head could go no higher, now his tongue was darting this way and that way. It had now found my pussy lips, in, out, in; his tongue was now inside me as far as it could go. "Oh yes Paul that's so good." I told him. "Paul give me your dick, now, oh now, please Paul." He withdrew his tongue, now he was standing up behind me, he soon freed his eight inch dick from his trousers, and it was now rubbing along my pussy lips looking for the entrance. "Oh God yes, oh get it in" I begged him. Then all of a sudden he rammed it inside me with much force. This took me by surprise, because I had relaxed my muscles, and the force with which it entered me made me a squirt out some pee. Now not only could I feel his dick going in and out I could also feel my pee trickling down the inside of my leg. I soon sensed his pending orgasm was approaching fast, I tightened my muscles to grip his dick even tighten. He let out a groan. "Yes, yes, yes," his whole body tensed and stiffened, and then he was pumping his sperm into my now dripping wet pussy. "Stay there," I told him my right index finger was searching for my clitoris and as soon as it found it I started rubbing it fast, up and down, this way and that way. Now it was my turn, for my body, to tense up and stiffen, because now, my orgasm was washing over me.

Later that night when we were both lying in bed, I asked Paul about going on holiday. "Paul have you ever been sailing, I mean on a boat, not at sea, but cruising on the Norfolk Boards." "Well no what would we have to do?" "We just hire a boat for a week or so live on board and cruise along the waterways." "I would not have thought that was your sort of holiday, the Judy I know would rather be lying under the sun in Spain drinking white wine all day long." "Well I don't mean for our main holiday I just meant for a short break, that's all Paul." "Well I'll try anything once, as you very well know." He told me.

CHAPTER FOUR

Robert and Julie Baker, plus their only daughter called Donna, who had just started school at the beginning of the year, were looking forward to their holiday. Julie Baker considered herself lucky. Really, she had left it too late before booking the boat for the holiday, particularly as it had to fall in the school holidays. She was however lucky one boat was still available, and that boat was 'pretty Emmylou'. How pleased she was as she showed the picture of the boat to Robert and Donna, that evening.

Julie's life with Robert Baker had not been an easy one. In the past, way back in his, 'dark days' as Julie called them; she could not believe what he was capable of doing. Even Robert himself could not believe the, 'dark things' he had done. Especially to the only Woman, who he, had only, ever, really, truthfully ever loved and cherished. Julie pushed the recollections of Robert's, 'dark days' to the back of her mind. After all why should looking at a picture of the boat they were to go cruising on, remind her of all those bad, unforgettable 'dark days' reminiscences?

Donna was holding the brochure, she was looking at the picture of the boat, Julie had shown her. Julie realized she was staring at it for longer than a five year old should. "So Donna do you like the boat we are all going to go and live on, when we all go on holiday?" Again Julie realized she was taking too long to answer, for a five year old. When Donna did answer, it made no sense to Julie or Robert. "Daddies going to go and live on that boat for ever and ever and we will never ever see him ever again." Julie gently took hold of the top of the brochure, and slowly pulled it out of Donna's small hands. "No, don't be silly darling when you and I come home from the boat, then so will Daddy." Then, acting more like a five year old, Donna jumped Up, off from the floor, and started to run around in a circle and started to sing, "Ring-a- ring of roses, a pocket full of poesies, who's going to be brave, to save Daddy from he grave?" Robert and Julie just looked at each other, and wondered just where their five years old daughter had heard those words before.

Later that night when Donna was tucked up snug and warm in bed, so was her Mother and Father, in the next room. Julie however could not forget her daughter's words. "Ring-a-ring of roses, a pocket full of poesies, who's going to be brave, to save Daddy from the grave?" Julie dug Robert in the ribs, "What do you think she meant Robert, when she sung that song tonight?" "It was nothing, she didn't even understand what the words meant, she was just singing them that's all, nothing more, nothing less." "I just hope you're right

Robert, I just hope you're right." And on that note they both drifted off to sleep. However it was not a dreamless sleep for Julie.

She was crouching down in a corner, hugging to her chest a frightened and sobbing daughter. She was unaware of where they were, it was some kind of a 'dark' wooden shed or room of some sort. She was sure she had never been here before. By the moon light pouring in through a round window she could make out the outline of a man. A large drunken man, holding an empty glass bottle, high above his head, and ready to strike. She soon realized it was herself and her frightened sobbing daughter that he was aiming for, oh yes, aiming for with the empty bottle.

"Julie, Julie wake up," now it was Roberts turn to poke her in the ribs. Julie was glad to be woken from her dream well from her nightmare really. "What is it-" Julie began, and then she heard what it was. It was Donna crying out in the middle of the night, a very scared and a very frightened Donna. Julie jumped out of bed as quick as she could and went rushing into Donna's bedroom. "Mummy's here darling, its alright everything is alright." she reassured her daughter as she sat herself down on Donna's bed. Donna fell into Julie's strong warm arms, and tried to stop herself sobbing. After a good five minutes at last her sobbing subsided. "Did you have a nasty dream?" Julie asked her. "No Mummy it was not a dream, it was real, a real man, we were hiding, from him, but he found us." "Don't be silly darling what man, who was he?" What Donna said next made Julie's blood run cold. "It was Daddy and he was so, so very cross at us. He wanted to kill us. Mummy is Daddy still cross at us now?" "No, no darling Daddy is not cross at us now, he is fast asleep in bed, and he would never ever do anything to hurt us, never." Even as she spoke she prayed that, what she had just told her daughter was true.

After Julie had got Donna settled down and, back to sleep, she tried to do the same thing herself. However she tossed first this way then that, and the sleep she so desired still eluded her. She asked herself if her daughter and herself had in fact had the same dream. And if they had, both had the same dream, what did it mean, if in fact it meant anything at all.

Next morning at breakfast found Julie and Robert sitting, facing each other over the kitchen table. "Robert" Julie began "this boat trip, do you still think it is such a good idea?" "Yeah why not, you can't cancel it now, just think how disappointed Donna will be." "Well I think she was having a nightmare last night about, about, Well I don't know what it was about. It's just that I have a bad feeling about it, that's all." "Julie everything will be just fine and dandy you just wait and see." replied Robert. Not only was Robert trying to convince Julie, he was also trying to convince himself. For he, had also been dreaming last night.

During the day it was still playing on Julie's mind, so much so she even phoned the boat yard to see if they could swap boats. Unfortunately, they told her, that was the only boat available, and that 'Pretty Emmylou' was one of their newest, and finest boats of the fleet. Donna however had seemed to have forgotten all about last night, and all about the nightmare.

All too soon, for Julie anyway, the school holidays were here, Robert was busy loading up their red, eight year old Vauxhall, which had seen better days. All that was left now were two cardboard boxes of groceries. Robert bent down to pick up the first one and froze, when he saw what was inside it. The box was full of bottles of Brandy, Rum, Vodka, and Whiskey. That's not to mention cans of Lager and Cider. What the hell he thought, where did this lot come from. He looked around to see if Julie had seen he was about to pick up the box. Julie had banned all kinds of alcohol from the house, some five years ago when Donna was born. Robert had never really forgiven her for that. These days alcohol would have been his only pleasure, but as always Julie knew best. Or at least she thought she did. And of course she had no way of knowing how much she had made him suffer, these last five years. In those last five years, not one day, had gone by, when he was not craving a drink, not one day. Of course she thought she was so clever, she thought she knew best. *"But does she?"* A small inner voice said in the back of Roberts mind. *"But does she?"* When Robert saw Julie was nowhere in sight, he wondered if he could get away with having a quick one, after all she would never know. But when he turned back to the box, all the booze had gone, and the box was now full of the grocery supplies. *"What the hell is going on? Now I'm seeing things am I going crazy?"* Before he had time to answer himself, Julie appeared at the kitchen door way. "What have you been doing," she demanded, "I thought those boxes would have been in the car by now." "Just doing it now my dear, just doing it now."

At 11:00 that morning the Baker family were all in the car and were heading towards Olton boards *"Well*

Robert what good is she really?" The voice was so loud and clear in Roberts head; he thought Julie had spoken to him. He turned to look at Julie, "Sorry what did you say Julie?" "Nothing Robert I didn't say anything, just keep your eyes on the road." *"Yes Julie I would also like to keep my eyes on that box of booze that was in the kitchen this morning."* Except of course it was never even there to start with, it was only there in Robert's mind. *"Well Robert, just what is her problem, depriving you of a little drink, what harm could it do, to a big strong man like you?"* The same sexy female voice asked in Robert's head. "ROBERT LOOK OUT" shouted Julie. Just in time Robert saw the young woman pushing a pram across the zebra crossing right in front of them. He stepped on the brakes as hard as he could. The Vauxhall shuddered to a stop, with just feet to spare, stalling the old engine, as it did so. "ROBERT WHAT THE HELL WERE YOU THINKING ABOUT? Didn't you see that woman, crossing the road? You could have killed them both." "Then they were lucky it was not raining, if it had been raining we would have skidded and we would have just mowed them down for sure." And a wide grin appeared on Robert's face. "Robert I can't believe you just said that, what is wrong with you today." *"Tell her Robert, Tell her there is nothing wrong with you, that a quick drink won't fix, go on tell her."* Instead Robert just looked at Julie and shook his head said nothing. The young woman pushing the pram gave Robert one last dirty look before stepping safely onto the pavement. "That was fun Daddy do it again" sang Donna from the back seat. "Donna calm down" scolded Julie, "That was not fun that was dangerous, or it could have been dangerous." Robert restarted the old engine, on the second attempt and continued to drive on. It was less than an hour later the family drove into the car park of the boat yard. The look on Donna's face when she saw all the boats moored up by the side of the river was a picture. "Mummy, Mummy, is that one our boat, look, that one over there?" Julie looked to where here daughter was pointing. "We don't know yet, not until we see the boat man." Deep down Julie had a very bad feeling, a very bad feeling indeed. What she really, really wanted was to just get back into the old Vauxhall that had brought them here. And just go straight home again.

Roger was in full Saturday flow, he had his tour speech down to a fine art. Of course he knew it, off by heart, after all he should have done. He gave this speech about fifteen times every Saturday. It was as he showed the Baker's around their boat, he was sure he sensed too different kinds of moods here. Mrs. Baker was uptight, her whole body moved with stiff movements. Where as Mr. Baker was, was well, relaxed, and at home. As if he had lived on this boat for years, and as if he would never, ever want to leave this boat ever again.

"Yes the name on my Master card is Mrs. Judy Andrews." "Well thank you very much Mrs. Andrews, that's all gone through for you, the boat 'Pretty Emmylou' is booked for your family for one week, commencing Saturday 11th April. We look forward to seeing you then, Goodbye, and thank you once again." I put down the phone, and I wondered if I was doing the right thing. But I was sure there must be some kind of story here somewhere. What kind of story I didn't know, I had told Paul nothing about the history of this fairly new craft, as told to me by Roger. I think I just wanted him to come along with an open mind.

"Wow" said Robert, "will you two just look at that sunset." Julie was not impressed; Donna on the other hand wanted to know if the sun was falling out of the sky? They had been cruising down the river now for a good three hours, and Robert who was the pilot was looking for somewhere to moor up for the night. Just up ahead in the distance was a long line of boats all moored up. The reason for this was a large old public house set back from the river. "This looks like a good place to moor for the night he told Julie." "I don't know, do we really want to spend the night outside of a boisterous pub?" Julie wanted to know. "How do you know it's boisterous?" replied Robert. Before she could answer the boat seemed to make up its own mind. The throttle lever moved itself to the neutral position. With the engine on tick over the boat started to slow down. "Look did you see that? The boat wants to stay here the night as well. Looks like you are out voted, on this one, my dear." "Don't start being silly Robert, that's where Donna gets it from." "Ok now Julie remember what Roger told you about mooring, you go and stand on the bow of the boat right at the front, and hold on to he mooring rope. When you are close enough to the bank jump off the boat and onto the bank, and tie up the mooring rope to the mooring post. Everything was fine, and going according to plan. The bow of the boat was edging nearer and nearer to the river bank. Julie got ready to jump, with mooring rope in hand. Julie was poised and ready, but the very moment before she bent her knee's to jump, the throttle lever moved itself to full power with the engine in reverse. The boat now started moving backwards. By the time Julie realized what was happening it was too late to stop herself, from jumping. As she jumped she screamed as she became aware that the gap was now too bigger a gap for her to jump. With a great big splash Julie landed in the muddy cold river. "HELP I CAN'T SWIM" Julie was shouting at the top of her voice. Robert tried in vain to shift the throttle lever, back into neutral, the boat by how had put a good maybe thirty feet distance between themselves and Julie. Then all of a sudden the throttle lever did allow Robert to move it. The problem was the lever was not happy to stop in the neutral position. It's moved itself past neutral and onto forward at full power. No matter how much force Robert used on the lever it just would not budge. The boat was now aimed at Julie splashing about in the river with the throttle lever stuck fast on full power. By now a small group of fellow boaters who had been sitting around a wooden picnic table outside the pub, drinking. Who, had all seen what had happened, had all rushed to the river bank with an orange life belt. Julie however was now in a state of panic. She could not feel the bottom of the river with her feet. Time and time again she would go under, splashing her arms and legs about trying to keep afloat. The small group of fellow boaters threw in the life belt to her. But her eyes were full of the dirty muddy water, she could not see, her ears were also clogged as well and she could not hear the group shouting at her to grab the life belt. One of the fellow boaters had to help her. He quickly took off his new trainers and jumped into the river to help the woman in distress. He was too busy trying to get the nearly drowned woman into the life belt to hear the high revving engine fast approaching them both. He also did not hear the warning shouts from his mates on the river bank. Warning him about the out of control boat which was now heading straight towards them both, at a top rate of knots. Robert was helpless he tried steering the boat away from the bank but the boats wheel was jammed he could not turn it in any direction what-so-ever. The boaters on the river bank were now concentrating on trying to save the woman in distress and their mate. Two of them laid front down on the edge of the river bank with arms stretching out trying to first reach, and then pull them both out of the river and on to the safety of the bank. The one with the longest arms just managed to grab hold Julie's fingers pulled her quickly to the bank and with the help of his friends pulled her up onto the grassy river bank. Their friend who was still in the water looked and saw just in time the speeding boat heading straight towards him. He however had no time to clime up onto the safety of the bank. The speeding bow of the boat was just four feet away from him surly it would crush him against the bank. Just in time he twisted his body in the water and kicked his feet. This action moved him five feet over to his left. Then just twenty seconds later the bow of 'Pretty Emmylou' crashed into the rivers bank. Robert could see what was going to happen, he was however powerless to prevent it. As the bow struck the bank the boat gave up. The throttle lever moved back to the neutral position, and the boats wheel was again free to turn. The group on the bank was helping a soaking wet Julie to her feet. The one guy in the water who had nearly been crushed had climbed out of the water and was standing on the bank shouting at Robert. "WHAT IN THE NAME OF BLUE THUNDER ARE YOU TRYING TO DO. YOU BLOODY IDIOT YOU COULD HAVE KILLED US BOTH." "I'm sorry really I am, there is something wrong with the boat, the throttle got jammed, and the wheel would not turn. I'm just glad you are not hurt." You're not are you?" "No thanks to you, no I'm not hurt.

Now about three hour later, Julie had, had a warm shower and she and Donna were watching a TV program. Robert had decided he was going to visit the pub which they were moored up outside of. "Where do you think you are going Robert?" Julie demanded. "I just thought I go and have a quick drink in the pub." was Robert's reply. Except Robert knew there was going to be nothing quick about it at all. "Robert what in the world are you thinking about, you know very well we don't drink now, do we?" "Well you might not my dear, but as for me; I've got just one thing to say to you, and that is, SOD OFF." Robert checked he had his wallet stormed off the boat and headed in the direction of the riverside pub. "Mummy, I'm scared," began Donna, and hugged Julie even tighter, than she had been doing so before. Julie was thinking about her options, the car was parked way back at the boat yard. How would she and Donna get there? If she could get to the car she could drive them both home. All she was sure of, it was not safe to stay here. Robert must not find them both still here. God alone knows what he would do to them both when he came back inebriated. Julie decided the best plan of action was to walk to the main road phone for a taxi to take them to the boat yard and collect the car. She could have called the taxi from here. But she had no idea how long it would be before Robert came back. Julie did not even stop to pick up a bag, just their coats and her purse, and phone. Then tugging Donna by the hand led her to the cabin door. Julie reached out for the knob but before she even touched it, she heard the double click, of the lock locking itself. "What the hell?" Julie said out loud. She still grabbed the knob anyway, hoping against hope that it would still open anyway. But deep down she knew the cabin door would not open. Next she looked around for a porthole or window big enough to crawl through. But unlucky for Julie and Donna none were. The only way out was this cabin door, which had been firmly locked. But by whom or what Julie didn't know. She rushed into the boats galley looking for anything she might use to break the lock with. But all she could find was a large carving knife. Julie grabbed it; if it would not break the lock she could use it to defend herself and Donna with. And defend herself and Donna she would. Even if it meant to the death. She had made up her mind, if she had to kill Robert to save Donna she would. "Donna I know lets play a game of hide and seek shall we?" Julie pulled some cushions from the bench seats and dropped them onto the cabin floor under the dining table. "We can turn off the light and hide under the table, Daddy will never find us under their will he?" Except of course she knew that he would. As Julie sat in the dark hugging Donna to her, the dream she had, had, came back to haunt her. She remembered this is what they had both been doing in her dream, or rather in her nightmare.

Robert had at last met the sexy lady whose voice he had heard in his head earlier. She was sitting on the bow of the boat waiting for him. She was the most beautiful woman Robert had ever seen. Her hair was fine and golden and was nearly so long it reached down to her waist. *"Hey sailor boy you going to buy me a drink or two?"* She wanted to know. "Why you just try and stop me." He told her. So together they walked into the bar of the Riverside pub. They walked to the far end of a nearly deserted bar, pulled out a couple of bar stools sat down and Robert ordered two drinks. A bottle of red wine for the new love of his life, and a double Whiskey for himself. "Shush, shush, Brian, come over here a minute, check out the weirdo sitting at the end of the bar." "Well, what's wrong with him Pauline?" Brian had been the landlord of this Riverside pub for the last fifteen years. Pauline was one of his best barmaids. Pauline whispered, "Well I've seen people talking to themselves before, now, but I've never seen anyone talking to someone who is not really there." "Pauline I don't understand what you mean." "He thinks he's with and talking to a real woman, hell look he is even buying her drinks. The strange thing is someone is drinking them. I'm sure it's not him drinking them himself. So who the hell is?" "Pauline I've told you before about drinking in the afternoon, remember, and you said you would not let it happen again. As long as he has the money he can buy drinks for all the ducks on the river, see if I care." Robert however was having a great time; at long last he had met the woman of his dreams. Here he was sitting in a bar next to the long golden haired, sexy young female. For the first time in his life he was in love. Really in love, this was the real thing this time. Ok so when he first met Julie he thought yes this is love. But he was wrong; he just thought it was love. And now that real love was tapping him on his shoulder, he was going to make sure it didn't get away from him. Now he was getting very drunk, but it didn't matter his new love of his life still kept buying him drinks. Robert was looking forward to taking her back to his boat and making wild passionate love to her all night long. Then he remembered Julie, yes that rotten cow Julie was still trying to ruin everything for him, still trying to spoil all his fun. Still trying to stop him from drinking. And now still trying to keep him from his new lover. Well he had now had enough, of her interfering in his life, but that was soon to come to an end. Because, he was going to put an end to it once and for all. Robert looked at the near empty wine bottle sitting on the bar just in front of his new lover. Mmmm that might do he thought to himself. He then cast his eyes over the all the other bottles lined up on the shelves all round the bar. They came to rest on a bottle of Jack Daniels fine scotch whiskey. It was not however the contents he was interested in. No it was the shape of the bottle which he, was interested in. It was square, yes square would be good and the whiskey inside would be good also because that would add a bit of weight. "Bar tender, bar tender, sell me that bottle of Jack Daniels." *"Please"* added his lover. "Sorry, yes I meant to say please." Robert picked up the Jack Daniels, they both left their bar stools behind them and staggered out of the pub and into the bright moon light. Then they both started singing at the tops of their voices.

"Show me the way to go home,
I'm tired and I want to go to bed,
I had a little drink about an hour ago,
And it's gone right to my head,
No matter where I roam,
Over land or see or foam,
You will always hear me singing this song,
Show me the way to go home."

They had now arrived at Robert's new home. Robert turned to face his lover, "now you just wait here for me, there are just two little things I have to take care of first ok?" Those two little things he was referring to was Julie and Donna. With his Jack Daniels firmly held in his hand he stepped aboard his boat, he stepped aboard his new home.

Julie had no idea how long they had been hiding under the table in the dark. What she did know was she was dying for a pee. What she was hoping was, Robert would come back so drunk he would just pass out, and forget about her and Donna. It was Donna who first heard him singing, she hugged Julie tighter in response. They listened as he grew nearer and nearer. Then they could hear him talking to someone. A shred of hope entered Julie's mind. Just maybe he had met someone in the pub, and had brought them back here, for, well, for coffee, or something. Maybe they would be saved, after all. The double click of the cabin door unlocking itself made Julie and Donna jump. The door burst open, and having a hard job to stand up in the door way was Robert with a bottle in his hand. He stood there letting his eyes grow accustomed to the darkness. "Come out; come out, wherever you are." Robert half said and half sung. "Don't make me angry you won't like me when I'm angry." *"Hurry up Robert its cold out here, and I just can't wait for you to take me to bed with you"* "I'm sorry lover; I will be as quick as I can." Robert said out loud. Julie looked all around but she could not see who he was talking too. Maybe if Donna had not chosen that very moment to sneeze he would never have found them. But sneeze she did, and find them, he did. Robert bent down so he could see underneath the table. A wide grin appeared on his face. "Come on out here my dears, so that Daddy can smash your heads in with a Jack Daniels. Julie thinking the best form of defense was attack started crawling out from under the table, telling Donna to stay put, where she was. "And who do you think you are talking too?" Demanded Julie. "Just look at the state of you, Robert go to bed, now Robert, go to bed now." Julie had however pushed too hard. "The only place you two are going to is hell" laughed Robert. Julie now stood facing him about five feet away. "Robert I'm warning you, just take one more step toward me and so help me God, I'll cut off your useless balls." And just to back up that last statement she waved the carving knife about in front of her. Robert roared with laughter, "You stupid cow you did that years ago, when you took away all my fun. Years ago when you stopped me from drinking. Do you remember that, when you stopped me drinking. Well I remember that. And I have never forgiven you for that. Well Julie from here on in I do whatever I like, and you my dear, have stood in my way for the very last time."

Robert took one step forward. "NO ROBERT STOP, PLEASE STOP." Robert took another step forward. Julie knew she had to do it, and had to do it now. Her right hand held the carving knife real tight, she aimed the point of the carving right at his beer gut, and plunged it forward, as hard as she could. Due to the fact Robert was drunk his reactions were well slow. Which meant he was too slow to fend off the attack? At first Julie was not sure if she was strong enough to push the knife through his tough skin. She pushed still harder, his skin gave way the knife then slid in easy, in it went in deeper and deeper. Until nearly all twelve inches were buried in Roberts guts. Warm blood was now washing over Julie's hand; she froze in shock at what she had just done. She let go of the knife's handle and took three steps backwards. She was holding her clean hand over her mouth and screamed for all she was worth. Thanks to all the drink Robert had consumed he felt not a lot of pain, in his guts. So he just left the knife where it was still buried deep inside himself. So with Julie frozen with shock he took his chance. Robert raised the square Jack Daniels high above his head, aimed it at the side of Julie's head and brought it down as hard as he could. The bottle found its mark with a dry thud, and then just bounced off. Julie stopped screaming, and for what seemed like forever just stood there. Then at last her knees started to buckle, if she was still alive which was not, but if she was still alive she would have felt the warm trickle running down her legs as her bladder emptied. Yes Julie was well dead before her whole body hit the cabin floor. Robert however was not sure if she was dead or not. After all the crafty cow may have been pretending to be dead. So that he would leave her alone. But Robert was not that stupid, not by a long chalk. So just to make sure he knelt down next to her and started to bash in her head. He knew for sure if her head was flat then she would be dead for sure. Time and time again down came the Jack Daniels, Julie's skull bones began to shatter. Bits of bone were now sticking out of her face, and an eye ball went rolling across the cabin floor. Robert was pleased with his work. Julie's face was now well flat. She was dead now for sure. But now Robert had lost far too much blood he was growing weaker and weaker. He was so tired all he wanted was to sleep. So he laid down next to Julie on the cabin floor. Which came to Robert first sleep, or death, is something we will never know.

The God fearing couple in the next boat moored next to 'Pretty Emmylou' heard the screams. They had to go and investigate. They found the boat to be in darkness. As they peered in through a window they heard a small, scared child's voice singing, "ring-a-ring of roses a pocket full of poesies" but the song was never finished, the small voice just sang that one line over and over again. She was still singing it in the ambulance on her way to hospital. The bodies of Julie and Robert were never found, only the blood covered cabin floor, and a full bottle of Jack Daniels.

It was Roger who was given the task of going to the Riverside pub. To collect the boat. After the police had finished with it of course. All roger knew was a little girl was found on he boat and taken to hospital. The cabin floor was covered in blood and both the parents had disappeared. After he returned to the yard and had cleaned the floor, well the best he could anyway, he went to see his boss. So let me get this straight Roger "you want me to burn a perfectly good craft, because you think its haunted or something." "Well it must be" said Roger every time people hire that boat out something bad happens. That boat has been nothing but trouble, even when it was being built, it was nothing but trouble." "Now Roger this is what I want you to do, I want you to listen to me and listen real good. Do you understand?" Roger nodded his head. "We will never burn that boat, we will keep on hiring it out, and there will be no more talk about that boat being haunted, to anybody. Now Roger do I make myself clear?" Roger looked down at the office floor, "Yes sir boss I understand." As Roger walked away he wondered who he could turn to for help. And the only person he had spoken to about that boat was the newspaper woman. Now what was her name?

The tabloid woman Roger was thinking about was me, I was at this very moment sitting at the bar of the Riverside pub. In fact I was sitting in the very same spot Robert had sat in a few nights before. "That man was well weird," Pauline was telling me. "He was acting as if he had someone here with him. He was talking to them, asking them questions, hell even buying them drinks." "So who drunk those drinks, did he?" "Well that was well weird as well, not once did I see him drink any of those drinks, but he still kept buying more when 'his friends' glass was empty." Brian the landlord walked past Pauline and caught part of the conversation. He looked at Pauline then at me. He then rolled his eyes, "I keep telling her to take more water with it. Does she listen?" "So did he say anything about the boat?" I asked. "No, nothing that I heard anyway" replied Pauline. "I do remember late afternoon a group of boaters came in talking about a boat being out of control, and how it could have easily have killed someone. But I don't know which boat they were talking about.

As I was driving myself home, once again I asked myself if I was doing the right thing in hiring that boat for a week. And maybe I should warn Paul of its history.

The next day was dull and overcast as I parked my red BMW in the newspaper office car park. Mike was already at his desk, tapping away on his computer. As I walked into our office Mike looked up, I could feel him undressing me with his eyes. And why not, I was wearing a green trouser suit, hiding a matching set of a sexy lace bra and panties, in Mike's favorite colour yellow. "So" Mike wanted to know, what did you find out at the Riverside pub, yesterday?" "Well nothing really, the barmaid said a group of people came in talking about a boat that was out of control, that was in the late afternoon. On the night it happened they had in some creepy guy who was with his best friend, except his best friend was invisible. But that did not stop him from drinking, his best friend I'm talking about." "Do invisible people drink?" Asked Mike. "Well apparently this one did." I said. "It just does not make sense, if the people who hired this boat are in fact dead; if they have been killed somehow then where are the bodies? That's what I would like to know. "Well I don't know," began Mike. "But what I would like to know is what colour underwear are you wearing today." "Mike shut up and be serious its only a few days before Paul and I go on that boat, and I'm not sure if we should still go now, what do you think?" "Judy it's a boat, what are you suggesting, are you suggesting, like what's his name, Roger that it's haunted? Judy, we have had haunted houses, haunted hotels, cars, castles, ships, but not a pleasure craft, well as far as I know of anyway." The phone on my desk started to ring, with one last look at Mike I picked it up. It was Sally the receptionist. "Judy" she began, I have a Roger here to see you, he won't give his last name, but he does say you know him." "That's ok Sally I'll be right down." I replaced the receiver and adjusting my left bra strap headed down to reception. Roger was nervously pacing the reception floor, "Roger" I said walking over to him holding out my right hand, "what can I do for you?" He ignored my right hand, "What can you do for me? He asked, you can start off by listening to me, that's what you can do for me." "I'm sorry Roger I don't understand," "Oh you don't understand, well, I saw them, I saw the booking sheets for 'Pretty Emmylou' I saw you're name Andrews, Andrews that is your name? After all I told you that boat is well bad, it's haunted or something. Do you remember? I warned you never to go on that boat. Something real bad happens to people who hire that boat, and something real bad will happen to you, that's for sure. I've said what I came to say now I'm going, before someone sees me here." With that he turned and rushed out the main double doors, before I had finished saying. "No Roger please wait, come back let's talk about this.

When Roger arrived back at the yard he saw two police cars in the car park. He looked down to the riverside where 'Pretty Emmylou' was moored. His boss Stan Clark was standing by the boat talking to two policemen. Inside the boat inspecting it again, with the engine running was the same marine engineer who had inspected the throttle lever and the boat before. Roger decided to go and find out what was going on. "Ah" said Stan as Roger approached, this is all part of the police investigation regarding the missing parent's of the little girl. People, who were at the Riverside pub that day, contacted the police saying they saw this boat that afternoon completely out of control. One woman who we believe to be the mother, fell in the river, someone jumped into help her and nearly got crushed by this out of control boat. The man, who we believe to be the father, told them the throttle lever and steering wheel got jammed and was stuck solid. So the police are inspecting the boat for a second time." "Have they found anything yet?" Asked Roger. "Not as yet, so far it has a clean bill of health. Roger turned to the policeman and said. "You don't need an engineer for what you are looking for here. What or rather, who you need here is an exorcist, someone who can carry out an exorcism on this boat." Stan laughed, long and hard and said, "yes very funny Roger, These officers don't want to hear your stupid jokes." The policeman however did not laugh, because they were both thinking the same think. They both thought Stan's laugh went on for far too long, it was also a false empty laugh. The policeman with rather a large protruding nose, turned to Roger, and asked. "Why do you think we need an exorcist sir?" Stan butted in, "he doesn't its just Roger saying stupid things like he does all day long, Roger has nothing at all to say about this boat. Do you Roger?" Stan then gave Roger such a glare, the sort of glare that said Talk and you walk, in other words, remember what I told you. You don't talk to anyone about 'Pretty Emmylou'.

CHAPTER FIVE

"Paul," yes sugar, Paul sometimes called me sugar usually just after we have made love. "Paul I haven't been completely honest with you about next week, when we are on the boat." "Mmmm I wondered when you were going to get round to telling me." "Tell you what?" "Oh come on you are taking your lap top, note pads, pencils, why would you be taking all that stuff if it was just a short break?" "Well yes I may need to make a few notes. But Paul its not that, well not just that, anyway, it's the boat." "What's wrong with the boat it looks fine in the brochure," "yes and it is a fine boat, but Paul it's always in the news." "Well then that's ok then, because you my love will be right their, pad and pencil poised, you will be able to give a first hand account of whatever it is that's going to happen, won't you?" I lightly bit down on my lower lip; Paul came over to me and wrapped his strong arms around me, and held me tight. My breast's pushed against his chest; I could feel his stiff penis pressing against my crotch. I slightly parted my legs and felt his erection bury itself deeper into my crotch. Our lips met and we shared a long lingering kiss. Our lips parted, "first one naked on the bed goes on top," I said. On top was my favorite position trouble was it was also Paul's as well. Our bodies parted we both made a dash for the stairs, undoing buttons and things, and discarding items of clothing as we went. I just happened to jump onto the bed about four seconds before Paul. He did not complain but lay down on his back just like a man should. I straddled his erect penis, took hold of it and guided the head to the entrance of my eager, moist, waiting and ready vagina, I slowly lowered my body down, down all the way down, until his penis was buried good and deep, inside me. Paul reached up with his hands and started caressing both of my bare breasts. I started rising up, up and stopped just before he was about to pop out, I then quickly bounced back down as quick and as hard as I could. I had only been doing this for a few minutes when I sensed Paul's fast approaching climax. "Not yet Paul I pleaded, wait for me." I reached down with my right hand, my index finger soon found my clitoris I started rubbing it up and down slowly at first, and then I quickened the pace. "Oh yes Paul, oh yes, oh yes, here it comes Paul, yes it's coming. Oh my god Paul, yes, yes, yes." My climax washed over me, and I collapsed down on top of Paul. We then just lay there like that, not moving I could feel his slowly shrinking penis inside of me, and wondered at the magical delights of the human penis.

On that Saturday morning we were both awoken by the sound of thunder. It must have been right overhead because the lightning and the ear shattering clap of thunder happened both at once. I remembered as a small girl I would count the seconds in between the lightning and thunder and however many seconds you counted meant the storm was that many miles away. "Today of all days, and you chose today to start our boat trip." Mumbled Paul, "Paul it's just a little storm, it's going to be fun, you'll see."

We were about halfway through packing our bags, when the knock came at the front door. I glanced at the hallway clock. It told me it was dead on ten o'clock. I was nearest to the door so it was me who opened it. Standing on the wet door step was a person who at first glance looked to be a gypsy, or at the very least a nomadic looking old woman. She was huddled up in an old thick woolen patch work coat, with every other button missing. "Yes can I help you?" I asked. As the rain poured down. I looked into her deep lined weathered face. But it was the eyes that caught my full attention; it was her eyes that I could not tear my own eyes away from. Her eyes were crystal clear, amber in colour and so deep, and so very, very beautiful, much too beautiful to belong in this world anyway. "No my child you cannot help me, but I can help you. Give me your right hand." I slowly offered her my right hand after only a moment's hesitation. Her hands were all wrong to belong to an old woman. They were too big, and they were too strong. They were also deformed. But not in a repulsive way as they should have been. Both the warm strong hands covered my right hand and held it tight. For the first time I could see why her hands were deformed. Both hands had a hole going right through from one side to the other, in the middle of her palms. The old woman's face was now looking up at the sky. She started talking softly, so softly I could hardly hear what she was saying. However the words I could hear were not English words. She was talking in some kind of strange foreign language. I could feel warmth, warmth that started in my right hand, and slowly spread up my arm until the sensation invaded my whole body. It was peaceful, calm, warmth like, such I had never experienced before. Now I could feel something warm and hard in my hand, what it was or where it had come from I just didn't know. Now the old woman looked back at me, "You and your husband must wear these at all times. If you don't you will be in much danger." As she spoke she slowly released my right hand. I looked down, and there in the palm of my hand I saw two bright gold, shining crosses on chains. I looked up and started to ask, "who are-" but stopped in mid-sentence. The old woman had gone, I rushed down our front path to the road, although I looked up and down the road, she had gone, and gone without a trace. As I headed back towards our front door, my first thought was, what am I going to tell Paul? I also thought about just opening a draw somewhere and just dropping both the crosses into it. Then I realized, when the old woman had said, "you and your husband must wear these at all times." it was not a request, no it was more like a command. A command I felt I could not disobey. "Who was that at the door?" Paul wanted to know. So I just told him the truth. "It was a sort of old gypsy woman." "Well what did she want, money I suppose," he went on." "No Paul she did not want money, she just wanted us both to wear something." Paul looked at me from the corner of his eyes. "Oh what, did she want us to wear?" "These

Paul, she wanted us to wear these." I opened out my hand and showed him the two crosses. "Feel them Paul they are still warm." "Course they are, you have been holding them in your hand." "No Paul feel them, it's a special sort of warmth, not what I would call human warmth. It's warmth not from this world." Now he was looking at me out of the corner of his eye again. "Judy for God's sake will you listen to yourself, what the hell are you talking about?" I took two steps closer to Paul and put my left arm around his waist, and kissed his cheek. "Please Paul I know I'm not making much sense, but will you please just humor me, just this once, and you have no idea how pleased you would make me, by wearing this cross?" He looked at me, long and hard, I tried to guess what he was about say. "Well its no big deal, sure I'll wear the cross if that's what you want me to do." "Oh Paul I do, I do," I then kissed him long and hard full on the lips. I did however pull away when I felt him try and force his tongue into my parted lips. I had banned tongues from my mouth way, way back in the seventh, grade at school. When during a biology lesson, we were told that million and millions of nasty germs live on our tongues. And Paul although I love him dearly, I didn't love the millions and millions of his tongue germs. I then reached up with both hands, and slipped the cross and chain over his head. The cross landed and rested on his hairy chest, just below his neck. Paul reached up and felt it, "feels warm to me, and that's it. That's all I feel, it's just warm, that's all, nothing more, nothing less. From the look on his face I could see how much pleasure he took informing me of that fact.

Some four hours later found us driving into the

boat yard car park. Paul left me sitting in the car while he went to reception to book in. It was not long before he returned with Roger. As they both approached the car I released the seat belt and climbed out of the car, into the now bright sunlight. "Judy this is Roger he is going to show us over the boat," announced Paul. "Yes" I began, "we've met before, how are you Roger?" Roger charged right in, ignoring my greeting. "I was hoping you had cancelled, but its not too late you know you still can." "Cancel why would we want to do that?" asked Paul. Roger looked at me, so you haven't told him then? "No Roger I didn't tell him about all that superstition nonsense you believe in, now are you going to show us over the boat or not?" Roger shook his head, then after just a moments hesitation turned and said, follow me please. We walked behind Roger as he led us down to the riverside and all the moored up boats. Roger stopped next to a boat, well here she is 'Pretty Emmylou' your fine boat for the next week." Although the mooring ropes were well loose the boat gently bobbed up and down close to the bank. Roger stepped aboard, turned and reached out his right hand, for me to grab hold of, as he was going to help me aboard. I stood close to the edge of the bank reached out my right hand, grabbed hold of Rogers and held it tight. However just as he started to pull, and, just as I lifted my right foot to step over the gap between the bank and the boat. It was at that very moment the boat started to drift away from the bank. The gap was growing wider and wider until at last the mooring rope grew tight. It was lucky for me Roger let go of my hand otherwise I would have been in the dirty water of the river. Roger pulled hard on the mooring rope until the boat was back where it had started from. "What the hell happened then?" Paul demanded. "Why were the mooring ropes left so loose?" Roger explained, "when you moor up a boat the mooring ropes are left loose on purpose. This will allow the boat to rise and fall with the tide. You just need to be careful getting on and off that's all." Once we were all aboard Roger was now having trouble with the cabin door, well to be precise the lock on the cabin door. No matter which way Roger turned the key, no way would it open. "That's strange" said Roger, "I've never had any trouble with this lock before." Then Roger understood what was going on here. "I know what it is, it's you two, and this boat does not like you two, that's what it is." "Roger" I began, "yes, yes, I know talk and I walk." Paul looked at me with raised eyebrows; I just shook my head, thus telling him to leave it alone, and not to ask any questions.

Eventually somehow Roger managed to get the cabin door open and the rest of the boat tour and the rest of the day and that evening were uneventful, uneventful that is until bed time. That night as we were both getting ready for bed, Paul decided to remove the cross as he was getting undressed. "Judy undo the clip on this chain, please I don't want to wear it to bed." "Sorry Paul I don't think there is a clip." "Well there must be, how did you get it on?" "Well I just slipped it on over your head." "So in that case just slip it off me again then, simple." But try as I might the chain was now too small to fit over Paul's head. Not only that, but I found out, my chain had shrunk as well. Neither of us could take off the gold chains. "This is just bloody Stupid," Paul went on, "Gold does not shrink, never did, and never will. Well until today anyway, and on this Godforsaken boat." "Paul just shut up and come here and warm me up in this bunk I'm freezing cold."

That first night was when we both had the same dream. Or should I say nightmare? We had both been fast asleep in the boats double bunk, for a good few hours.

I realized I was short of breath, why I didn't know. Something was tightly wrapped around my neck, at first I thought it was the thick body of a long snake, gripping my neck tighter and tighter. I grabbed the snake's body to try and pull it free. I then realized it was not a snake's body around my neck at all, no what was gripping my neck tighter and tighter were hands, human hands. But not just anybody's hands, no, these hands belonged to the man that I loved, they belonged to Paul. "Paul" I tried to shout, "Let go of me," but as in most dreams or nightmares, no sounds will come. I then became aware of a heavy weight lying on top of me; with his feet he was now forcing my legs apart. His stiff penis was pressing hard up against my vagina. All the while his hands still gripped my neck blocking my wind pipe. I tried shouting again, "Paul you dirty bastard get off of me, this is rape Paul-" I then gave up because still no sound would come. I then saw Roger's face, and heard his words, "never go on that boat, something bad always happens to people that go on that boat." Next I saw two people splashing about in the river, just by the bank. I heard the roar of the engine, but above the roar of the engine I heard laughter, yes laughter. The boat was laughing as it headed at full speed towards the two people splashing about in the river. As I looked in the water I could now see things floating around in the water. The once muddy water around the boat had now changed to a bright red colour. I looked and saw a hand, floating on top of the small waves, and to the left of that was an arm. A human head floated past the hair was all disarrayed, as it floated just underneath the surface. The open eye balls looked straight at me. What was this? It was a foot, and yes I think that was half a woman's breast. The nipple just floating above the surface of the water. The same nipple that had been kissed so many times, when it was alive, and not always by men either. I had seen enough I opened my mouth to shout, "NO, NO, - NO, NO." Paul and I both woke up at the same time, we both sat up in the bunk, both of us trying to remember where the light switch was. Paul's hand gripped my arm, "Judy its ok it was just a dream," he tried to reassure me. I pulled away from him, "don't you touch me you dirty bastard, you tried to rape me, I was asleep and you tried to rape me." "Judy I swear I didn't it was all a dream, well all a nightmare. "So you tried to rape me in your nightmare did you Paul, was it a turn on for you Paul?" "Look Judy calm down, are you saying we both had the same nightmare?" "You had your hands round my neck, I could hardy breath, and then you got on top of me and tried to rape me. Oh Paul it was all so horrid and then I was looking in the river the water was red with blood. I saw a woman's body parts floating past by the side of the boat. And Paul the boat was laughing." Paul had by now found the light switch, and had got back in the bunk with me. "Oh my God" said Paul "that's the same nightmare I had, we both had the same one, both at the same time. I wonder if that has ever happened before to other people." I told him I had no idea, but I did start getting out of the bunk. "Where are you going?" Paul wanted to know. "I'll be right back just got to go pee." "Paul, Paul, come and help me the toilet door won't open, it's stuck somehow." I stepped back to give Paul room, Paul twisted the door knob and it opened first time. Paul gave me one of his looks, out of the corner of his eyes, as if to say I was telling him porkpies. Paul went back to the bunk; I sat thankfully down onto the toilet seat. It was then I heard the lock of the toilet door give a loud click. That did not bother me, what did bother me was when I tried to unlock the door the lock was jammed fast. "PAUL, PAUL" I shouted, "I'm locked in the toilet, come and help me please. No reply so I started banging on the door. "YES, YES, I'M COMING." "Judy if you are messing me about, I'll just have to bend you over my knee pull down your yellow panties and give you a good spanking." "No honest Paul it really is jammed. And try as he might Paul couldn't undo it either. "So what do we do now?" I asked, "Well Roger did say if we had any trouble ring the yard, but I don't think he meant at three o'clock in the morning." I looked all around, the toilet and the shower unit was all in one, with just one small port hole for a window, and I couldn't even open that, because that was jammed shut as well. Then all of a sudden I thought that I must be dreaming again, because right before my eyes, the shower mixer tap started turning itself anti-clockwise. Round-an-round it unscrewed itself until the tap was wide open. Water was now flooding out of the shower head and filling the shower tray. The tap then just fell off the shower unit, and landed in the shower tray. "PAUL GET ME OUT OF HERE, THE SHOWER IS ON FULL, AND I CAN'T TURN IT OFF. AND NOW IT'S STARTING TO FLOOD THE FLOOR." "JUDY LISTEN TO ME, SWITCH ON THE SHOWER WAIST PUMP SWITCH, REMEMBER THE ONE ROGER SHOWED US." The water was now about six inches deep, I paddled across to the waist pump switch, and flicked it to the on position. The loud bang and flash that came from the switch made me jump well back. "NO PAUL THAT'S NO HELP, DO SOMETHING ELSE." By now the water was up to my knees, and rising all the time. "HOLD ON JUDY I'LL SMASH THE LOCK WITH THE FIRE EXTINGUISHER." I could hear Paul bashing the lock with the extinguisher. "PLEASE, PAUL HURRY, THE WATERS UP TO MY THIGHTS NOW." Although Paul was bashing the lock as hard as he could it made no difference what-so-ever the door refused to open. By now the water level was up to my breast's, the thought hit me, I'm going to drown in here, I now started to panic, real bad, and still the water was rising well fast. Before long the water was up to my chin, and that was standing on my tip toes. I then felt something, something warm around my neck, it was the cross and chain, but why would it get warm now? Maybe it was reminding me it was there. Maybe it was, but what good was a cross and chain to me now, even if it was a warm one? I was now standing up on the toilet seat; the top of my head touching the ceiling, I figured there was maybe 12 inches of air space left. The cross around by neck was getting warmer and warmer, what did it mean? My panicking mind made the connection, the cross a representation of Christ, of God, Easter, Christ died on the cross; three days later he overcame death and rose up from the grave. If I was to overcome death I had to overcome this door, but how? I took hold of the now hot, cross in my left hand, and reached out and held it up in front of me. The chain which before had shrunk now felt like it was on elastic. "PAUL" I shouted, "YOU'RE CROSS, HOLD THE CROSS UP AGAINST THE DOOR." Between me and the door was maybe about five feet, five feet of water, which I had to swim, across to the reach the door. I took a really deep breath and pushed myself up and off the toilet seat that I had been standing on. I had done perhaps two or three strokes but it was like swimming through sand. I could then see why, floating around in the water in front of me were about four or five, nameless faces. Faces which had no bodies. And it was they, who were blocking my path. As the first nameless face appeared right in front of me I held up the cross and stabbed at the face with it. In an instance the face just vanished. I repeated this another four times. But by now I had no air left in my lungs. I knew this was my last chance I had to reach the door with my last stroke, or drown here and now. My last thought before my cross reached the door was, I sure hope for once in his life Paul will do what I told him to do. Lucky for me he had, as I pushed the cross against the door, without hesitating the weight of all that water flung the door wide open. I was gasping for breath even before I collapsed into Paul's waiting arms.

"Paul I think That Roger was right all along about this boat." We were both sitting at the cabin table drinking a mug of hot coffee. After we had both stripped off our wet clothes and gotten ourselves dry. "He said he thought this boat was haunted, but I'll go one better than that, I think this boat is evil, yes Paul I think this boat is nothing but pure evil." "Oh come on Judy don't you think you're overreacting?" "OVERREACTING, overreacting, Paul this boat tried to murder me half an hour ago, and you dare ask me if I'm bloody well overreacting?" "Look Judy, the toilet door got stuck, ok, nothing more nothing less." "Oh yes and the showers tap turning itself on and then falling off. And the faces floating about in the water trying to stop me reaching the door, just how do you explain that, Paul, well?" "Ok look Judy first thing in the morning I'll phone the yard, get that Roger over here. He can mend the shower tap, fix the sticking door, and everything will be fine." "Paul don't you understand there is a lot more wrong with this boat than a broken shower, and a sticking door." "Well then that's ok because Roger will be able to fix anything else you can think of when he gets here, can't he?" "No Paul he can't because at first light we are taking this boat back to the yard, getting our money back and then going home. That's what we are going to do."

So at first light that's what we did, we raised the anchor, untied the mooring ropes and cast off. We turned the boat around and headed back down stream to the boat yard. Not long after we moored up back at the yard our boat was the only one there, all the other boats had been hired out. At this time it was still early, no one had as yet arrived for work. As it was a nice day we sat down on the river bank to wait. Or rather I did, not wanting to go back aboard that boat I sent Paul back onboard to fletch our bags. However after about fifteen minutes had gone by Paul still had not come back. I got up and walked down to the boat calling Paul's name as I went. I stood on the bank next to the boat looking in. Or at least I tried to look in, through the portholes. I realized for the first time the porthole's were blacked out, and wondered why I had not noticed that fact before. But what I happened to see laying discarded in the newly cut grass of the river bank, was Paul's cross and chain. Why, he had decided to take it off, I don't think I will ever know. But taken it off he had. "PAUL" I shouted, "PAUL COME OUT HERE NOW." I waited, and listened for any kind of acknowledgement, that he had heard me. No, nothing, I was sure he must have heard me. The very last thing I wanted to do was to go back on that boat, but it seemed I had no choice. "MRS. ANDREWS," it was Roger calling my name, I turned to see him hurrying to join me. "What is it? What's up? Why have you come back?" Roger wanted to know. "Oh thank God you're here Roger, I'm sorry, I owe you an apology, but first please go on that boat and make sure Paul is ok, I've been calling him, but it seems he can't hear me. "Oh why do you owe me an apology?" asked Roger. "No please Roger later, first make sure Paul is ok, now please." At last he understood the urgency, for without further ado he climbed aboard the boat and entered the cabin door. If I had been watching the portholes, which I wasn't, but if I was I would have noticed they were no longer blacked out. It was a good ten minutes before Roger slowly emerged from the boats cabin, try as I might I could not read the expression on his face. I shook him by the arm, "Roger, what is it, tell me, is Paul hurt?" "He is not hurt, well I mean to say, not the sort of hurt you can see anyway." "Well where is he?" "Oh he's still on the boat; he's just sitting on the floor in the corner under the table singing." "Singing, singing what for God's sake?" I demanded, "he's just singing the same line over and over again. Ring-a-ring of roses a pocket full of posies." "Roger has the cheese slid off of your cracker?" I demanded." "No Mrs. Andrews, not my cheese slid off my cracker, but I think your husband's cheese has slid off his cracker, good and proper." "Roger listen to me, I want you to go back aboard that boat and tell my husband to come out here right now, and don't take no for an answer." "I will go and try but I don't think he can hear me." Roger turned on his heel and once more jumped aboard 'Pretty Emmylou.' "Good morning Madam, my name is Stan Clark I'm the yard manager, is their a problem here, can I help you in anyway?" I turned to see a tall slim grey haired man wearing a suite holding out his right hand for me to shake. I ignored his out stretched hand, looked him fair and square straight in the eye and asked of him. "What the bloody hell do you think you're doing hiring out this? this, death trap?" "I'm sorry I didn't catch your name." "My name is Andrews, and my husband and I are the poor sod's who you hired out this death trap to." "Well Mrs. Andrews I'm sorry to see how upset you are, why don't we all go to my office so we can sort this out. "Sort this out, sort this out, Mr. Clark not five hours ago your boat tried to murder me, it was only thanks to this cross around my neck that I didn't drown, and as for my husband, right now he's sitting on the floor under the table singing some bloody song, over and over again. And I want to know just what it is you are going to do about it?" We now both turned to see Roger rematerialize from the boat. Once again try as I might, I could not read his facial expression. "Well" I asked impatiently, where is Paul?" "I'm sorry I was talking to him, but he just looked right through me as if I was not there." Stan reached into his jacket pocket and took out his mobile, and dialed nine, nine, nine. "Ok Mrs. Andrews I don't pretend to understand what's going on here at the moment. But first things first, we are going to get your husband checked out, then I'm sure we can get to the bottom of all this."

Chapter Six

However two weeks on, and Stan Clark still had not got to the bottom of everything like he had said he would. As a gesture of goodwill he did give me a full refund. But with Paul still in the mental hospital, a refund was the last thing on my mind. He refused to believe that I, nearly drowning was instigated by the boat. When I pointed out to him the boat was evil, and haunted, he just laughed, and said, "Mrs. Andrews in once what was, Great Britain, we have had haunted houses, hotels, castles, Ships, even cars. But we have never ever had a haunted pleasure craft on the Norfolk boards." "Until now," I told him, "until now."

The day after that it rained all day, I took the day off work and went to the hospital to visit Paul. He had, at last stopped singing, which the doctor told me was a good sign. However Dr Greengrass also told me something which made no sense at all. Well not at first anyway. "Mrs. Anderson, if I was a Doctor who believed in human souls," he began "which, I'm not, but if I was, I would have to say, your husband has lost his soul." "I'm sorry," I said, "I don't understand." "Well some religious people believe the soul to be the spiritual part of a person that continues to live after the body has died. So take away the soul and all that's left is an empty body. An empty shell, if you like, a bit like a computer, with no hard drive, no memory, no files, no nothing." "Ok so can we, can he, ever get his soul back do you think, and if so how?" "Mrs. Anderson I did say, that I did not believe in the soul, but that does not mean, it does not exist, as for getting it back, that would depend on how he lost it, and where it is now." "I know where his soul is, that bloody boat has stolen it. It tried to steal my life, but failed, so it took the only thing it could. It took Paul's soul." "I'm sorry now it's my turn not to understand." replied the Doctor. I rose to my feet, held out my right hand, for the doctor to shake, and said, "when this is all over I will explain everything, but for now thank you so much, you have been most helpful, and now I know, what I must do."

The first thing I did when I arrived home from the hospital was to dial the boat yard number. It was answered on the fourth ring by a sexy sounding female voice. "Good afternoon," I began, is it possible to speak to Roger?" "Err yes who shall I say is calling," "nobody if you don't mind, I would like to surprise him." "Ok please hold I will try and find him for you." After a couple of minutes I heard an out of breath Roger say, "Hello Roger speaking, how can I help you?" "Hello Roger, it's Judy, Judy Andrews," I paused giving him a chance to say something, however when he didn't I went on. "Listen Roger I think you have been right all along about that boat, and I would like to meet you and talk about, what can be done about it." After what seemed like a pregnant pause, Roger at last found his tongue. "I don't want you calling me here, I don't want to be seen with you, if my boss finds out he will fire me, he will I know he will." "Please Roger, I didn't give my name just now, and I do understand, you are frightened for your job, but Roger we have to stop that boat before it goes on to murder God alone knows how many more unsuspecting holiday makers, don't you agree?" Silence, I gave him time to think. "But how, how can we, and we alone stop that bastard boat?" "That's what I want to talk to you about, Roger, can we meet in the pub again." "No not in the pub I might be seen." "Ok I'll come to your house, or you can come to mine." Again silence, I was just beginning to think I had pushed him too hard, when he said. "Give me your address I'll be round after work about 6:30."

True to his word at 6:33 Roger rang the door bell. I open the front door Roger took one last look around to make sure no one was watching him, and hurried inside. "Roger thank you so much for coming, let me get you a drink, I have a nice five year old bottle of brandy if you're not driving." "No I'm not driving; I didn't want my car outside your house, so brandy will do fine thank you so very much." I poured our drinks, and sat down opposite Roger. "So" Roger began "just what is it that you are proposing? Mrs. Andrews." "It's Judy, please call me Judy, I think you are right when you say the boat is haunted. It kills people but not only does it want lives, whatever it is, it also wants their very souls as well. It then stores up the lives' and soul's it has taken, and keeps them on the boat somehow. My question to you

Roger is, if we destroy the boat, or blow it up, or burn it, or whatever, will we save the lives and souls that are kept on board that boat? Or will we destroy those as well?" "I don't think it matters, one way or another, what's done is done, the boat has to be destroyed at any cost, we have nothing to lose." "I have, I have something to lose, Roger, I think the soul belonging to my husband, is held on that boat. And then of course if we get caught setting fire to a boat its arson, we could both go to prison." "Ok, ok I'm thinking," said Roger, "but while I am, my glass is empty." I got up and poured us both another large brandy. Which Roger downed in one. But I didn't mind the more he drunk, the more he talked, and the more he talked the more I was sure he was going to help me. "Gas bottles," he declared, "really all those boats are floating time bombs, and they carry a tank full of diesel, at least two gas bottles. It would be easy to make it look like an accident." "But where could we do it?" I asked "it would have to be well away from any other boats, and roads, we don't want the fire brigade turning up and putting out the blaze now would we?" "A little creek, about maybe two miles from here," Roger began, "no one ever goes there, that would be the ideal place." "But Roger if their are no roads near, to this creek, how are we going to get home?" "Simple, by another boat we both pilot two boats to the creek, blow up 'Pretty Emmylou' and come back home, in the second boat. See simple, I told you it was going to be simple, didn't I? And not only that I am going to tell you when we are going to do it as well. But you will need to pour me another drink first." I did pour him another drink, just before I burst his bubble. "But Roger the police will want to know who, and why, took the boat to the creek, in the first place, and how did they get back from the creek?" "Judy, Judy, Judy, you did say I could call you Judy didn't you? It doesn't matter, they, the police, won't know who took the boats to the creek, they won't know who to ask, and they won't know who blew up the boat. ""But, Roger what about finger prints, they may find your prints on an un-burnt bit of wood or something." "Well of course they would, I have to service that boat, of course my prints would be all over it. And it's going to be, well it has to be done this Friday night, I have finished the repairs to the shower and pump, the boat is booked out for the following week, comencing this Saturday, so we have to do the dirty deed, this Friday night." "But hold on Roger, surposing we do annihilate the boat, but we also obliterate Paul's soul as well, will that mean he will be an empty shell for the rest of his life?" "Judy, Judy, Judy, listen to me, he is an empty shell now, we have nothing to lose, apart from the fact that, I'm not sure if fire can destroy a soul, and I'm not sure if anyone knows the answer to that question. Anyway what makes you so sure Paul's soul is kept aboard that boat?" "I have seen the souls that live there, they were all floating about in the water when I nearly drowned, they were trying to help me drown," "I'm sure they were." "Yes Roger they wanted me to drown. Why, if it had not been for this cross, which they seemed to be scared of, well I would have drowned for sure."

But now sitting here on the toilet in the cold light of day, just thinking about last night had turned the contents of my bowl to liquid. There I was, yes little old me, who had never broken the law before in my life, not even a parking ticket. Here I was planning arson, planning to blow up a boat, it all seemed so unreal. I told myself I was doing it for Paul. I had nothing to lose, he is an empty shell now, and if his soul did burn, well then he will still be an empty shell. But on the other hand by burning the boat I would be protecting other people, and if Paul's soul did survive he would have me to thank. And not forgetting the boat will be insured anyway. Deep down, I just knew I was going to do the right thing. But I was still feeling uneasy, with just me and Roger, what if something went wrong, I then knew I would feel happier if someone else came along as well, but who? At long last I got up off the toilet, and wiped myself. After a nice hot shower, I looked in my wardrobe, I was looking for something smart and something sexy, in the end I settled for a tight knee length blue skirt, with a slit up the back. My top was an almost see through white blouse, and today I was going braless. As my legs had a good tan I left off my tights, and under my skirt just wore a lacy pair of yellow panties.

As I walked from my car in the office car park my nipples were soothingly brushing against the inside of my blouse, causing a slight sexual sensation. "Wow" exclaimed Mike, as I walked into the reporter's office. I gave him one of my nicest smiles. "My God Judy you look, well, stunning for this time of day. Mike's eyes were popping out of his head. "Good morning Mike, yes thank you I'm well, thank you for asking." "Yes I can see that, you look very well indeed." I sat down on the corner of Mike's desk. Showing him too much of an abundance of my tanned legs. "Mike," I began, "are you doing anything Friday night." "What this Friday, it's a bit short notice, why?" "Well we both have an assignment to cover, are you free?" As I said are you free, I made a point of slowly crossing my legs. I was not disappointed to see Paul's eyes taking a long lingering look. "What time he asked." still looking at my legs. "It's a night Assignment so say midnight." "Well ok but only as a very special favour to you." he wanted me to know.

It was not until we were both sitting at our desks at lunch time, that Mike asked me. "So then Judy this night assignment what's it about?" "Boats it's about boats." "Is it anything to do with the boat you hired out just before Paul was admitted to hospital?" "Well yes in a way it is." "But why then does it have to be done at night?" "Paul" I began, "if I was to tell you that this err, assignment was not strictly legal, and above board, would you change your mind about doing it?" "So when is anything, that you do strictly legal?" He asked me. I gave him a smile, "just one thing Mike this is hush-hush, between me and you, no one must know, ok?" "Judy trust me, I am the soul of discretion." "I think you will meet my expectations mike, but this will be done on a need to know basis, you will need to trust me ok?" "Err I think so, but you are starting to worry me now."

It was not until I was driving home from work that night that I felt the first prang of a guilty conscience. I had roped Mike into all this, he had agreed without knowing what he was getting himself into. Hell if it all went tits up, we could all be sent to some God forsaken penitentiary, somewhere. I decided as soon as I got home I would phone him and explain, just what it is we are going to do.

"Wow Judy, will you just stop right now, and just listen to yourself. Hey it's Paul who's in hospital having lost his marbles, and right now, I'm sitting here thinking you should join him. You will never get away with it, and even if you do, the police will investigate, and, that's not to mention the insurance company, who would have to pay out about a hundred thousand pounds. And the insurance company won't do that without a fight." "Mike" I said quietly "I know all that, but I have to try, for Paul's sake, I have to try. So if you don't want to go ahead with this I will understand, and I do apologize for trying to trick you into doing this dirty deed." "Ok Judy, let me sleep on it, and I'll let you know tomorrow." However for Mike tomorrow wasn't going to come. After Mike had hung up the phone he needed a drink and a stiff one at that. He looked in the fridge, in the drinks cabinet, nothing. Mike had now been divorced for about two years, and one of the last things his now ex wife had done was to throw away all of Mikes drinks. Yes ok Mike had been a heavy drinker, but he had also been a good husband, a good provider, hell he even made love to Sally nearly every night, even if he didn't want to. But even that was not enough to hold together their marriage. So just before Sally moved out she just poured all his booze down the sink. Mike picked up his car keys, and making sure he had his wallet closed the front door behind him. Mike did not usually drink and drive, but anyway just a quick one, won't hurt. Or that's what he told himself anyway. At eight o'clock that evening Mike drove into the car park of the Riverside pub, and killed his engine. Inside the bar there was maybe about three groups of, Mike was guessing boat people, having a meal and drinks, while leaving their boats moored up outside. Mike walked up the far end of the bar and seated himself on a bar stool. As chance would have it was the same bar stool that Judy had sat on some weeks ago. "Good evening sir, what can I get for you this evening?" Asked Brian the landlord. "I'd like a double brandy and coke, please mate." Mike responded. It was then Mike turned and saw her for the first time. She was the most beautiful woman Mike had ever seen. With long golden hair and the prettiest, come to bed eyes, that he would never see ever again, even if he lived to be a hundred, and one. Is this stool taken she asked Mike?" "Err no please sit down." Brian turned thinking Mike was talking to him. "Sorry sir what did you say?" "No I was talking to this young lady here." Brian looked and was surprised to see there was no young lady there. Their was no one there, Brian thought to himself, oh my God not another one, talking to an invisible person. Brian had by now poured Mike's drink. "Can I get you anything else sir?" he asked. "Yes thank you, you can get this young lady whatever it is she's having." "Err yes, and what might that be sir?" Mike turned to the young lady and asked, "what would you like to drink?" She replied, "*Why thank you kind sir I would like a bloody Mary, thank you so much.*" "Well you heard the lady, barman; it's a double bloody Mary. Brian poured the drink and sat it down on the bar, in front of the empty bar stool. He could not wait for Pauline to turn up for work, what would she make of it? As the evening wore on Mike and the new love of his life, were getting well drunk. "I don't believe this," said Pauline to Brian, shaking her head slowly from side to side. When she arrived at work that evening. Another crazy mad fool. Pretending to have an invisible friend, and by the way he's acting I'd say she was a female invisible friend, wouldn't you?" To his credit, time and time again Mike would say, "no more to drink," I've got to drive home, but this cut no ice with his sexy young friend. Mike was well looking forward to taking her home, and home to bed, for an all night sex session. Which he hadn't had for years. Well that is what she had promised himself anyway. He had wanted to call a taxi but the love of his life told him he was capable of driving and anyway she told him she couldn't wait to get home. And of course neither could he. So they walked out of the bar arm in arm, and went straight to Mike's car. Mike started the engine, he turned to his new lover, and told her, "I'm not sure about driving like this, everything is spinning around." *"Come on darling you will be fine."* She told him and at the same time rested her right hand on his aroused penis. Mike started to drive. The country road was only narrow but as Mike gathered speed the road seemed to get wider, and wider. *"Come on darling, faster, faster."* she encouraged him. Mike told himself he was well in control after all he knew the road, every twist and turn; well that's what he thought anyway. However just up ahead, with the Speedo touching eighty mph he entered a sharp left hand turn. The car handled the corner well, considering the speed, but Mike could not help drifting over to the right hand side of the road. He then blinked, and blinked hard, he could not believe what he could see just up ahead in the middle of the road. It was a boat, taking up the whole width of the road. Mike did not even have time to press hard on the brake pedal; he did not even have time to reach the brake pedal. Instead he twisted the steering wheel round to the right. "Yes" he just had time to say, as he just missed the boats hull. However he was now heading straight towards a great big oak tree which had been growing by the side of the road for about a thousand years. In his drunken state he had forgotten to fasten his seat belt, and of course his new love of his life hadn't reminded him to do so. His body was flung through the windscreen and he hit the tree head first. Poor Mike was killed outright. The coroners report, later reported that Mike had a blood alcohol level of well over 80%.

The next day was Friday, as I drove to work the sky was overcast. I hoped the cloud cover would disappear before tonight, so that we would have the moonlight to guide us down river to the creek, as the boats don't have any navigation lights. On the other hand I told myself, in the moonlight we might be spotted, by some idiot walking his damn dog or something. I realized I had arrived before Mike because there was no sign of his car in the car park. As I walked past reception I called out a cheery "good morning" without looking to see who the receptionist happened to be, that day. And then I made a beeline for our office. I could not wait for Mike to arrive to hear his answer. It was now 9.30 Mike was late, hell, Mike was never late. My thoughts were interrupted by the ringing of my phone, on my desk, on my clustered desk. "Hello Judy," I said into the phone. "Err hello Judy, its Mandy on reception," "Are you ok Mandy you sound a bit upset, is everything ok?" I asked. "Well no not really, Judy could you come down here please?" "Well yes of course Mandy I'll be right down." I dropped the phone back down and made my way down to reception. Wondering as I went whatever could be wrong. As I entered reception I saw two policemen talking to Mandy. As I approached they all turned to greet me. "Good morning I'm Judy Andrews I'm one of the reporters here, can I help you?" I asked. "Well we do hope so" said the younger good looking one with short black hair. "Judy its Mike" Mandy Interrupted, he's been in a bad accident," I looked at the two policemen waiting for them to confirm what Mandy had just told me. The young, good looking one nodded, "Is there somewhere we can go a bit more private?" he wanted to know. "Mike" I said "is he ok?" "We really do need to go and sit down somewhere to talk about this, he insisted. So I took them up to my office, once we were all seated, I asked again. "So is Mike ok? Is he in hospital? "Mrs. Andrews," the young good looking, started to say, "I'm so sorry, but there is no easy way to say this, his car was in collision with a tree, late last night, he was pronounced dead at the scene, I'm so sorry." "Oh my God I managed to say." I had to tighten my muscles quick, to prevent the flood gates of my bladder from opening. "Tell me," said the old, ugly policeman, were you in contact With Mike at all last night? You see we are trying to trace his movements, of yesterday evening." "Well yes but only by phone, but that was early on." "Did he mention anything of his plans for that evening?" Asked the old, ugly policeman. "Well no he didn't." I reassured him. Now the young good looking, asked, "was Mike a heavy drinker would you say?" "Why do you ask?" "Well early reports indicate a high level of alcohol in his blood." I shook my head, "no that can't be, Yes, he did like a drink or two, what man doesn't? But one thing he never, ever, did was to drink and drive, he was always adamant about that. He was always so careful; I remember the time just before his divorce. When he was hitting the bottle hard. He would phone me at home at eight o'clock in the morning, and ask me to go and pick him up, for work. He did not want to drive because he would say he had, had a skin full the night before. Just maybe he was not the driver; just maybe he could have been the passenger." "Well that is a possibility, and one, that we will be investigating." The young good looking, informed me. "Well thank you Mrs. Andrews, you have been most helpful, and again we are very sorry to bring you this bad news." Now I was alone with my thoughts, so tonight it was now down to just me and Roger. How it was all going to turn out I had no idea.

CHAPTER SEVEN

We had both arranged to park our cars at the Riverside pub. Go inside have a couple of drinks, and then walk from there to the boat yard. This would serve as some kind of alibi at least. While we sat over our drinks, I told Roger about Mike. He just shrugged his shoulders, it makes no difference he assured me, us two will be able to handle it, no problem. The look on my face told him I was not convinced, so he asked me. "Not having second thoughts are you," "No it has to be done, if not for Paul, then for all the other potential holiday makers, who hire that boat. Come on lets get going before I do get cold feet, I said to Roger. We walked out of the pub and headed down the road towards the boat yard. I must say I was glad I was not alone, walking along that dark road with woods and trees on either side it looked very, very spooky. It was me who felt it first, I stopped in my tracks and looked all around, Roger followed my lead. "Roger do you feel that?" "Feel what," he wanted to know. "Do you feel like we are being watched," I asked him. Roger took a long hard look all around us, but before he could reply trees and bushes began to rustle nearby, as if they were being blown by the breeze. The fact that their was no breeze, was lost on Roger. "Well Roger," I asked, just for a moment a smile appeared on his lips, "No its ok its nothing, lets get moving. At that point if I had looked at the front of Rogers trousers, which I didn't, but if I had a done I would have seen the bulge made by his eight inch erection. *"You can do it Roger, you know you can, and you know you want too. It will be easy, drag her into the woods grab her around her throat block her wind pipe, with your strong thumbs she will be dead in no time at all. Then you can rape her as many times as you like, no one will ever know it was you. Come on big boy before a car comes along and sees you."* Roger didn't need telling twice. He stopped dead in his tracks, turned to face me, and bent his back from his waist. His right arm went round the back of my knees; he now straightened his back thus picking me up in a fireman's lift. He then turned on his heels and carried me into the dark woods. I hammered on the bottom half of his back with my fists. "ROGER" I shouted, "PUT ME DOWN." he paid no attention to me what-so-ever. So I decided to try and humor him. I laughed out loud, "ok very funny big boy, but jokes now over, you can put me down here." He did slow his pace, but that was all, "PUT ME DOWN NOW, ROGER, BEFORE I SCREAM." Now it was his turn to laugh, and laugh he sure did. When at last he stopped laughing, it was just to say, "go on baby, you scream, and you scream for as long and as loud as you can. Every woman should scream long and loud just before they die." He then stopped, bent his back, released his arm from behind my knees and threw me to the ground in front of him. I landed on my back, which knocked the wind out of me for a moment. He then jumped on top of me sitting on my belly with his knees either side of me. Just as I was wondering what he was going to do next, his large workman's hand, found their way around my throat. My mind then had a flash back to my dream when we were on the boat. When Paul was trying to murder me. But that was just a dream, this was real, Roger was by far too heavy for me to push him off me, because he was blocking my wind pipe I could not shout or scream. I then felt something warm around my neck, it was the cross, I had forgotten all about that cross. I had worn it all this time; I had never taken it off. But now it was so warm it could have easily have burnt my neck. My right hand went in search of the cross, I told myself not to panic. My guess was I was twenty seconds away from blacking out. Just in time my finger tips felt the now hot gold cross, I clutched it in my fingers, then lifted it up till it made contact with Rogers's large, strong, suffocating hands. The effect it had was instant; otherwise I would not be alive to tell this story. His grip went limp, and he released my throat, I gasped in gulps of air, and for a few moments, that's all I could do. Roger straightened his back, took a look all around him, looked down at me, and wondered just where the hell he was, but more to the point, he did not know why he had me pinned to the ground. Straight away he started to clime off me. I then sat myself upright, "Judy" he began, "what happened?" As soon as I could talk, I said, "what happened, what happened, you Roger, you tried to strangle me here in this dark woods, that's what happened." Roger started to slowly shake his head to and fro. "No Judy I never would do that to you, honestly, never, I wouldn't." "Roger look at me for Gods sake, what would you call it then." Roger then took a few moments thinking, "I'm sorry, it was her, it was not me, I promise you it was not me." "Her Roger, who is her," "I'm sorry I don't know her name she lives on the boat, I'm sure she does, and she talks to me, not much, but I'm sure it's her." "So what did she tell you to do to me, then?" I demanded. "Well, well, she err, told me to...." "Come on Roger tell me the truth, you are in enough trouble as it is, if I was to go to the police and tell them you dragged me into the woods." "Ok, ok, but I didn't want to do it, really I didn't." "Roger just tell me." "She told me to, well strangle you, and when you were dead, she said, well, she told me, I could, well, rape you as many times as I liked. There, I've said it, that's what she told me to do; you have to believe me, do you?" "Yes calm down Roger I do, she, or it or whatever she is, knows we are a danger to her, she is trying to stop us getting to the boat, she wants to stop us from destroying the boat." "So what do we do now?" Roger asked. "We have one weapon, one tool, and for some unknown reason that weapon is this cross, for without it I would have drowned weeks ago aboard that boat. I have Paul's cross at home, Roger before we attack that boat you must be wearing it. It's the only way we can stay safe, it's the only protection we have." "But Judy, it has to be tonight, that boat is hired out from tomorrow to some unsuspecting family for a week, tonight is our last chance, our last chance to get rid of that boat. Does it have to be a gold Cross, does it matter what it's made of?" Roger wanted to know. I told Roger I didn't know, which was the truth, I didn't. "Maybe we could make a cross out of sticks," said Roger, "oh yes and what about the chain what could we make that out of, then, just tell me that?" "I'm not sure the chain matters; after all it's the cross which is the powerful, well the powerful weapon. After all if I remember rightly at Easter time, Jesus Christ died for us, nailed to a Roman wooden cross, that cross was made of wood not Gold. Then, Christ overcame death, for us, and on the third day he arose again, so that, who-so-ever believed in him would never die, and would enjoy eternal life forever more." Roger was looking at me, looking for guidance; I didn't know what to tell him. It was then that the cross around my neck started growing warm. I looked around, was I in danger? I raised up my right hand located my cross around my neck and wrapped my fingers around it, and held it tight. But it felt wrong, yes it felt warm, but it felt sort of too big, sort of out of shape, What was happening to it I didn't know. I looked down at it and slowly uncurled my fingers. Now I was getting scared, I didn't know what kind of force was at work here, for my gold cross and chain had multiplied. Instead of just one cross around my neck, now their were two. "Wow where did you learn to do that?" Roger wanted to know. When he saw the two crosses around my neck. "Roger I don't know who or what gives this cross its power, but the power of this cross is more powerful than her, or whoever or whatever, her, happens to be." I took hold of the new cross and chain and removed it from around my neck. I then held it out at full arms length, and indicated to Roger to bow his head, which he did.

"There you are Roger never take it off, I know it will keep you safe, come hell or high water." "Thank you I will wear it all the time." "Good now come on lets get going we have been delayed for far too long already, don't you agree?"

Before long we were both heading down stream Roger was the pilot of 'Pretty Emmylou' I followed behind in the boat yards breakdown launch. There was not enough cloud cover, to hide the moon, which meant we would be able to be seen too easily. But that was a chance we would have to take. After about half an hour Roger steered his boat down a narrow river off to our left. This in turn led up to the creek; once we arrived there we moored up the boats a good five hundred yards apart. Roger gathered the tools he needed, from the launch, which was just a spanner and a throw a way lighter, and a cloth rag, and an empty milk bottle. His plan was a simple one, he would loosen the fuel line at the bottom of the diesel tank, he would let the boat flood with the contents of the tank. He would then half fill the milk bottle with diesel; poke in the cloth rag half way in, the half sticking out of the bottle was the fuse. He would light the fuse, then throw the home made fire bomb into 'Pretty Emmylou' and watch her burn. How he was looking forward to watching her burn. However as Roger made a move along the river bank towards the boat, the boat had other idea's. As Roger got closer he could see the mooring ropes that he himself had tied loosely, were now pulled taunt. The boat was straining on the ropes trying to pull itself free. Roger started running I ran behind him, following him. "Hurry," he called to me "we can't let it get away."

When we got to the boat Roger was panting well bad, he was also holding the top of his left arm with his right hand. "Are you ok Roger?" I asked. He took no notice of my question, instead he said, "Quick, help me pull on the mooring rope, got to get the boat nearer to the bank, so I can jump aboard." At last we managed to pull the boat close enough for Roger to jump aboard. Once on board Roger stopped and turned, "Judy retie the mooring line, ready for me to get off again." he ordered. I grabbed the line pulled on it as hard as I could till the boat was touching the bank. I then tied it as tight as I could to the mooring post. After about ten minutes Roger staggered out of the cabin still clutching his left arm. I asked him again if he was ok, and if he had flooded the boat with the diesel from the full tank. He stepped ashore and sat quickly down on the grass bank. "I, I, think I'm having a heart attack, but got to finish the job first." "No Roger," I told him "we need to get you to a hospital, and fast. As I spoke a dark cloud, a storm cloud drifted over to hide the moon. I then realized we were perhaps miles from a road. "Can you walk Roger? We need to get you back to the launch, and then to the nearest road, and fast." Roger struggled to his feet, "ok but first get the bottle, light the fuse and throw the bottle on to that boat." We got back to the launch and I found the bottle where Roger had left it with the rag half sticking out. "Quick Judy look, look at that boat." Roger had sat himself down on the grass bank and was looking at 'Pretty Emmylou'. I looked; the boat was bobbing up and down pulling this way and that way trying to break free of the mooring ropes.

"Quick Judy we must not let it get away." And not

too far away in the disance we both heard a loud clap of thunder. "Quick Roger give me the lighter," Roger let go of his left arm long enough to fumble about in his pocket for the lighter. After what seemed like an hour he found it and handed it to me. I started running back to 'Pretty Emmylou' with the lighter and the milk bottle. Up ahead the boat was going wild, it had broken free of the mooring rope at the stern and was trying to do the same with the bow mooring rope. Then just for a moment everything was illuminated as bright as day, and that was closely followed by another loud clap of thunder. I had just got to within throwing distance of the boat; I flicked the lighter wheel, once, twice, three times. Nothing happened, no spark nothing. Then on the forth attempt, a small spark, followed by a half inch flame. I held the flame to the bottom of the rag fuse, at first I didn't think it was going to light, but after a couple of moments it started to burn. "WAIT" shouted Roger, "DON'T THROW IT YET." I stood there holding it as the flame on the fuse got bigger and fiercer. The boat in front of me raised itself up about five feet out of the water, and finally broke free of the last mooring rope which held her. She was now free, and was making a dash for safely. I had to throw the bottle now, before the boat got out of range. I raised up my right arm to the throwing position, took aim, and threw the bottle as hard as I could. I stood there holding my breath, just for a moment I thought the bottle was going to hit its target and land on the boat, but then at the last second, it just seemed to drop like a stone. It landed in the water about a foot short of the boat. All I could do was stand and look. I was also sure I heard that boat laughing, laughing at me, and laughing at Roger. Who I was sure was having a heart attack. Here I stood I had to admit defeat, I turned to look at Roger, he was no longer sitting up on the bank. No he was lying on his back motionless, I started running towards him. I knelt down on my knees next to him, "ROGER, ROGER," I shouted. No response, nothing. I slapped his face a couple of times, nothing. Now I have had no first aid training but my fingers found his pulse, at least I think they did. Nothing, no pulse, no rise and fall of the chest, his heart had stopped beating, Roger was dead. Now I'm not sure what happens to people when they die, some believe in Heaven or hell. If you have been good through this life then you go to Heaven, and will have eternal life. If on the other hand you have been bad, in this life, then you are sent to hell, for eternity, where you will find no end to your pain, and to your suffering. However, having said that, I once had two Jehovah's witnesses knock on my front door, and they held a different view. They told me, when a person dies, that's it, that person is dead. They are aware of nothing, and the body will decay over time. That is, until the third coming of Jesus Christ. When, he will remember everyone who has died, he will then 'restore' everyone, to their formal glory. He will rebuild the rotting body, he will remember their own personality, and they will be as new.   Every Christian will agree with the fact that Christ will return to this Earth sooner or later. And when he does the meek will inherit the Earth. And Christ will rule here, on Earth over man. I was now angry, I jumped up ran to the waters edge shook my fist at the boat which was now standing still about five hundred yards away. "YOU ROTTEN BASTARD" I shouted, "HOW MANY MORE LIVES DO YOU WANT, HOW MANY MORE SOULS?" The whole creek was then lit up by forked lightning, it started off high up in the sky, and zig zagged down and down, I then realized it was heading straight towards me. I crouched down low and tried to make myself look small, and braced myself, for God alone knows, how many thousands of volts, of electricity my body would have to endure. However in the end I needn't have worried, for at the very last moment the fork lightening steered away from me and scored a direct hit on the boat 'Pretty Emmylou.' I watched to see what would happen; at first I was disappointed because nothing did happen. The lightening died away, which was closely followed by an ear shattering clap of thunder. Then as I waited, the boat was then completely engulfed in a massive fire ball. The flames must have rose fifty feet into the air. Lighting up the entire creek and the surrounding country side. This was followed by two loud bangs, something round and heavy went flying through the air, over my head, which could have been a gas cylinder. Then as I watched the faces belonging to the souls held captive on that boat, were set free, the faces I had seen before in the shower floating in the water, the faces that tried to help me to drown. They were all floating up in the flames, being set free. The last face to rise up was the face of my Paul. I turned and ran back to Roger, and knelt down beside him. I shook him by the shoulders. "Look Roger, look, we have done it, we have destroyed the boat, we have set free the souls, who were held there, look Roger they are free. Of course Roger said nothing, how could he, Roger was dead.

I did feel well guilty about leaving Roger there lying dead on the grass bank, but there was no way I could have carried him on to the launch by myself. So all I could do was to take off my coat after emptying the pockets, and covered Roger's face with it. Besides which, the flames and the gas cylinders exploding would have been seen and heard by someone, somewhere. Therefore I stepped onto the launch started the engine, untied the stern mooring rope, took one last look at what was left of the burning shell of 'Pretty Emmylou' and headed back to the boat yard. I found my way back without any trouble at all, and tied up the launch where we had got it from, some hours before. I walked back past the woods where Roger had tried to murder me, or rather whatever lived on that boat had tried to murder me. My car was still where I had left it at the Riverside pub. After all that walking I was glad to at last sit down, in the driver's seat.

It was well getting on for six am when I at last pulled up outside my house. As I lay in bed waiting for sleep I wondered if Paul and his soul had been reunited yet, or even, could they be reunited, how would they find each other, again? Just maybe they would both have to go back to the same place that they were, when they were separated. That was my last thought before I was finally overcome by sleep.

Chapter Eight

I was awoken at ten o'clock the following day, as it was a Saturday, and it was mike's weekend on, that meant, it was my weekend off. The fact that Mike was dead, cut no ice with me. After a quick shower, I got dressed and made my way to the hospital to see Paul. How he would greet me I didn't know. The last time I went to see him, I don't think he even knew I was there. I walked into his room; he was just staring at the wall. He did not even turn his head to see who had entered his room. Maybe he just didn't care. So it was with apprehension as I walked first down the corridor, then knocked and knocked on Paul's door. That's strange I said to myself, I had in the past always found Paul in his room. And the door was never locked. Until today that is. What did this mean? I asked myself. I walked further on down the corridor until I came to the nurse's station. There behind the horseshoe desk, I found three nurses. One with a really large backside was bending over a filing cabinet, showing more leg than a nurse should do. Another one was reading a book, and the third one was filling in some kind of form. "Excuse me, my name is Mrs. Andrews, I'm here to see my husband, he's not in his room." I was expecting someone to look up at me, when no one did, I went on. I wondered if you had any idea where he might be." The nurse showing more leg than she should do said, without looking up, "Have you tried the day room?" "Well no, I'm not even sure Paul knows there is, a day room. "It's just down the corridor a bit further along, on the left hand side." She told me. I thanked her as I was walking away. In next to know time, I was standing in front of the door named 'Day Room.' I was just about to enter when I felt a gentle tap on my right shoulder. I turned to face a young man in his early thirty's standing in front of me wearing nothing apart from an eight inch erection. "Hey fruit cakes, want to get you're laughing gear around this." He wanted to know. I stopped myself just in time from giving him a good hard face slap. Instead I said "Get away from me you pervert." He thought this was funny, because he went running off down the corridor singing that line over and over again. "Get away from me you pervert" he sang at the top of his voice, Get away from me you pervert." I now turned back to the door marked Day Room, pushed it open and stepped inside. In one corner stood a TV set and arm chairs were scattered all around the room. With maybe three or four people watching the TV. Before I had time to take everything in, a familiar voice called out. "JUDY, JUDY, OVER HERE," I looked just in time to see Paul getting up from an arm chair; he walked towards me, with arms out stretched. We then fell into each others arms. Paul was the first to speak. "Oh my God Judy am I glad to see you, first of all where am I? Why am I here? And how did I get here? I just woke up this morning and here I found myself. Go and tell them you are going to take me home. "Ok Paul, ok, I'll go and talk to the Doctor." "Doctor, what Doctor," Paul wanted to know.

CHAPTER NINE

Now, yet again once more she was homeless. The fleeing, descending, nymph was lost yet again. She was searching, darting, and diving, first this way and then that. Time was running out. She and she alone knew who she was, or what she was. Or from whence she came. She had to find somewhere to take refuge, the dark was good. Yes, and so was the wood. The wood and the dark, she could almost hide away forever. Below her the river was cold and dark, it also lacked the shelter, she so craved, and the sanctuary she so badly needed. Then just to the side of the woodlands she spotted her new sanctuary, it was a half built house, the wooden roof timbers looked so inviting. In the years gone by, the Goddess had been regarded as very powerful, and very pretty, and one who carried great beauty. She wasted no time descending down into the wooden roof timbers. Wood was good, for she could make her beauty blend in with the wood. Her long flowing golden hair would become the woods natural grains. Her eyes and mouth would be as one with the natural wood knots. Her naked sexy body with dark skin would blend in very well. The nymph was as always very well hidden by the wood. With the human's naked eye, she could make herself elude detection. She was also growing hungry, hungry for souls, human souls. This is just what the builder Stephen Tonk's would find out for himself the very next day.

****

Book Two.

The Immortal Soul Of Mary Hickes

CHAPTER ONE

England 1700's.

George Lambert shuffled and limped, along the narrow dirty cobbled street, under an overcast sky, in his home town of Huntington. Under his arm he carried his canvas, easel, Paints and brushes. He was slowly making his way to the market square. When he at last arrived he looked around, and saw he was to be the first person of the crowd to arrive. Again he looked around, he needed to choose his spot carefully, not too near, or not too far away either. In the end he chose an old wooden bench seat on the far left, and about two seats from the rear. This would be a mighty fine spot to set up his canvas, and easel. In reality, from here he would have a really good view of the potential crowd, which would soon start to congregate. And also a really good view of the metal 'hanging chain' which was suspended from an old wooden 'A' frame, which was built standing on a square wooden stage, with four wooden steps leading up to it. George looked up at the sky and softly cursed under his breath; if it rained he would not be able to paint. He was starting to regret entering into this arrangement with the Hickes woman, or as some called her 'witch Hickes' her real name was Mary, she of course denied that she was a witch. George was not sure if she was telling the truth, or not, after all only a witch could fore tell the future. Mary Hickes did fore tell she was going to be arrested, and would have to stand trial at the assizes for practicing witchcraft. After all George told himself if she was not a witch, she could not predict the future now could she. The trial of Mary lasted just one day, the assizes found her guilty as charged, and she was sentenced to death by hanging. And that is why George

Lambert was here on this day, which was Saturday 28th July. He sat himself down on the wooden bench he had chosen and set up his easel and canvas. He remembered that night very well, the night he had first met the Hickes woman. He was drinking in his favorite ale house, and was completely under the influence. His work was hung all around the walls. The landlord took pity on him and would sometimes take a picture in return for all the ale George could drink in an evening. He now found his tankard empty for about the twelfth time that evening. He rose up from his seat, and was staggering across to the bar, with his empty tankard in hand. Without warning the ale house door burst open, and a drunken, staggering, singing woman rushed in, and collided with George. They both ended up in a heap on the saw dust covered floor. "Whoooppp's, I'm so sorry sire to have felled you to the ground, like this." she looked and saw his empty tankard on the floor, thinking it had been full, when she knocked it from his hand, she offered to buy him a refill. They both staggered to their feet, brushing the saw dust from their dirty dusty clothes. The woman picked up his tankard and told him "follow me kind sire to the bar, and I will replenish your tankard." "You have no need to do any such thing," George assured her. "But sire I am insisting that you will allow me to undo my wrong which I did to you." "In that case then thank ye kind madam, I will allow ye to replenish my tankard." As they stood at the bar it gave George time to look her over. She had black and grey shoulder length hair, a pretty face, with the brightest blue eyes that you had ever seen, all this however was spoilt by her smile. When she smiled, what teeth she had left were nearly black. George however tried to ignrore this fact, and his eyes travelled down the rest of her body. He was pleased to see her long black dress did not hide her ankles which were dressed in black stockings. George did like ankles which were dressed in black stockings.

He guessed as best he could at the size of her breast, although well hidden by her dress, they must have been at least a 39 inch. George did like 39 inch breasts. What man didn't he wanted to know. "Its you, its you," Mary shouted with glee. While holding out the now full tankard towards George. "What is me?" Asked George. "Ye, ye, done all these paintings, ye are an artist. Can ye paint I? "Of course I paint anything." "Do you paint the dead, or the nearly dead?" She wanted to know. Yes I paint anything." "What about me, what about a witch?" And that is how it all started. They took their drinks and sat themselves down at a corner table. "I want to commission a painting, a painting of me, a painting of a witch, a painting of a hanging witch, a painting of my doom." Of course the first question George asked was, "how can you make me a payment? If you want me to do this for you, do you have any gold or silver to offer me?" "Look at me sire, I have a fine body I can offer you far more than gold, I can fore fill your wildest dreams, your wildest desires, your wildest sexual perversions, the pleasures of the flesh can be worth far more than silver or gold. My body will be yours and yours alone, for the duration of one whole night. ye can do anything to me, in order to fore fill your wildest sexual fantasy. Ye show me a man who could say no to that, and in return all ye have to do is paint a picture of me being hanged." So George told her, she could consider this to be a done deal.

Well that night she had more than fore filled her part of the bargain, sex with an normal woman from now on would be dull and boring, for poor old George.

By now the hanging crowd had started to arrive and to take their seats. George had started to paint the hanging chain, and the stage, he then turned and started to paint the faces in the gathering crowd. All too soon the whole market square was filled with people wanting to see someone hanged. George was then busy with mixing colored paints together. By twelve noon he was more than ready; his picture covered everything from the mass crowd, to the now still hanging chain. Then a silence filled the air, this meant the entertainment was about to start. The Hickes woman came walking into the square surrounded by about twelve guards. The lead guard led Hickes up the wooden steps and positioned her facing the front and the crowd about a foot behind the hanging chain. The other guards all stood around the wooden stage in a circle. George was busy painting all the guards around the stage; he had intended to leave the Hickes witch till last. George was painting as fast as he could, by now she had a black hood on her head, hiding her face and the metal hanging chain was around her neck. George was starting to panic he could not paint fast enough. At the very moment he finished painting the guards, he heard, rather than saw the guard pull the long wooden lever to open the trap door in the stage. A cheer went up from the crowd, George looked up to see the body of witch Hickes hanging and swaying from her neck, which held tight by the metal hanging chain. George dabbed his paint brush into a spot of paint that he had already mixed up, into the colour he needed. He had left the painting of Hickes till last. However as he raised his brush, he had the shock of his life. There on the canvas with her neck in the hanging chain, her feet dangling in the air was the image, in paint of witch Hickes. George could not believe his eyes; he knew real well he had not painted her, so how in the name of God almighty did her image get onto his canvas?

That very same evening found George in his favorite ale house showing the landlord his 'hanging witch' painting. How pleased George was when at last the landlord, agreed to hang his painting in exchange for nights free ale. The landlord was of course hoping to sell the painting, and make himself a handsome profit. Trouble was no one liked the painting, his drinking patrons said they felt like the painting was watching them, was spying on them, somehow. If the truth was known everyone who looked at that painting was scared of it, although no one would admit it.

CHAPTER TWO

England Present Day.

It had now been two years since Paul and I had moved to Hastings. I had been a newspaper reporter working for a small paper in the small Norfolk town called, Olton Boards. We had both always loved the seaside town of Hastings on the south coast. So it was a dream come true, when we upped and left Olton Boards, and brought a bed and breakfast guesthouse, in Hastings. Ok, so running a guest house would never make us millionaires, but it would support us and hopefully make us a small profit. Over the last two years in the summer months we were fully booked, the location right on the sea front helped. Most of the time we were hanging a 'No Vacancy' sign in the window. Yes everything had been fine, until that Tuesday. It was a Tuesday, the first Tuesday in July, and we were fully booked. One of Paul's pastimes was browsing around some of the 'old town' junk shops. The streets were narrow and clobbered just like the streets of hundreds of years ago. He would often come home with some old book, or old ornaments, or old tea pots, jewelry, anything which was cheap, and took his fancy. Yes everything was fine and dandy, until that first Tuesday in July. I remember it well I was in the kitchen preparing the vegetables for the evening meal. In walked Paul carrying something under his arm and wrapped up in brown paper. "Judy, Judy, Judy, just you wait till you see what I have here. I nearly missed it as it was hanging on the wall in the shop the wrong way round." "Why Robert, just why was it hanging the wrong way round?" I asked him. "I don't care why Judy, it's a famous painting by an artist called George Lambert. I got it real cheap as well. I thought we could hang it in one of the bedrooms, to sort of give it a bit of, well you know." "No I don't know Paul; I don't know what you mean. You tell me." Paul had by now unwrapped the old dirty, dusty painting. "Oh my God Paul, whatever is that smell." The smell I was referring to was coming straight from the painting. "Its ok, its ok" Paul informed me, "It just needs a bit of an airing that's all. I looked at the picture, it was dark and gloomy. It was a painting of some woman being hanged, and watched by a crowd of people. All under and overcast sky. "Paul we are not going to hang a painting like that in one of our guest's rooms. Besides just looking at it gives me the creeps, I don't like it, one little bit, and, I don't like the smell and more to the point, neither will our guest's." Paul could see my mind was made up, "Ok" he told me, "I'll hang it up in the garage, for now to air it for a bit." "Yes Paul, you just do that small thing," I told him.

During the next few weeks, the painting had slipped my mind. It was now nearly the peak of the season, and we were fully booked. It must have been a Friday because I had just returned from the cash and carry. As soon as

I walked into the entrance hall I smelt it, before I saw it hanging there. I saw red; Paul had waited till I had gone out and then hung that creepy painting in the entrance hall. I marched into the kitchen, "PAUL, PAUL, where are you?" I shouted. No reply, it was my guess he was keeping a low profile, and who could blame him? At last I found him, he was changing the beds in room five, ready for the new arrival of the Johnson family that same evening. "Paul what the hell have you done? You know very well I hate that painting, and yet you just go ahead and hang it any way, against my wishes." "You said not in a guest room, well the hall is not a guest room, is it?" "Paul you are just splitting hairs, and you know it, I want that painting taken down." Paul gave up, "yes dear let me finish doing this first then, and then I will take it down, my dear." "Paul don't patronize me, I mean it, I want that painting taken down." It was however unlucky for the Johnson's that Paul did not follow my orders.

The Johnson's arrived that evening, Betty Tony and twelve year old Richard. While they were signing in in the entrance hall, it was Richard who saw the painting. "Dad why has that woman got a chain around her neck?" "I'm sorry," I told them I'm waiting for my husband to take down that painting, I never did like it." "Oh I don't know," said Tony they did used to hang people in those days, you know. And that is what the artist was trying to record. "George Lambert, piped up Paul, he was the artist who painted that picture." "Wow" said Tony; it must be worth a fortune, where has it been all these years." Betty then interrupted, "Yes I'm sure it's all very interesting, but it's getting late, it's well past Richard's bed time." "Yes I'm sorry of course, Paul will help you up to your room with your bags, now don't forget," I reminded them "breakfast is served between eight and nine."

That very evening as the hall clock struck midnight, everyone in the house was fast asleep in bed. The old painting hanging on the wall, down in the entrance hall started to merge, started to blend in, started to become part of the wall itself. Now it was truly part of the wall, it started to expand, to grow bigger, and bigger until it covered the whole wall area. Now the painting was coming to life, the woman who was about to be hung was removing the chain from around her neck. Once free of the chain she walked down the wooden steps, off the stage and headed straight towards the Anderson's entrance hall. Once there she simply stepped out of the wall, and into the entrance hall. There she stood, she raised both hands above her head, she then uttered a spell softly under her breath, and this was to ensure the house remained asleep. The witch then walked slowly up the stairs and towards the Johnson's bedroom. As she entered the room, Betty and Tony were in a deep dreamless sleep. Only Richard was stirring. Witch Hickes walked over to Richards's bed, and placed her hand on his shoulder and gently shook him, till he became awake. "Who are you?" Richard asked. "Why Richard my dear, I am your fairly God mother, I'm going to take you on a little adventure, you do like adventures, don't you Richard?" Without further ado she pulled back his bed covers and took his hand and helped him out of bed. "Mum, is mum coming too?" Asked Richard. "No, no my dear mum needs her beauty sleep, but you can tell her all about it when you come back." They held hands as they walked down the stairs. Richard could not understand why, his fairy God mothers hand was so cold to the touch. When they reached the entrance hall, Richard could not believe his eyes. "Wow" he said "look at the picture; it's grown as big as the wall." "Yes my dear it has, and that's where we are going, come this way, mind the step my dear. With that the two figures stepped out of the entrance hall and into the wall and painting. The wall and the painting then returned to normal. Apart from the painting that is. The one small exception was that the crowd watching the hanging had grown by one. Grow by one small twelve year old boy called Richard, who now sat on an old wooden bench watching the hanging.

The next day Paul and I were rudely awoken by loud voices. "RICHARD, RICHARD, WHERE ARE YOU? I sat up in bed; my first thought was *what the hell are they shouting about?* I got out of bed and started getting dressed, I then realized I needed to pee and badly. As soon as I had taken care of that and finished dressing I left Paul in bed and went to see what the commotion was about. I found Betty Johnson still in her night dress, covered by a yellow dressing grown, marching about here there and everywhere. "Mrs. Johnson is everything alright?" I asked. "No it damn well isn't Richard is missing, his bed was empty this morning, where could he have gone for God sake?" "Mrs. Johnson I'm sure he will turn up, have you checked all the bathrooms?" "Yes, yes I think we have looked everywhere, and there is no sign of him anywhere." "Mrs. Johnson lets go and check the front door and see if it's still locked, if its still locked it means he is still in the house somewhere." She quickly followed me to the front door. Sure enough the door was still locked from the inside. "Well at least we know he's not gone outside." I told her. "Well then where the hell is he then, that's what I want to know, and I want to know now?" It was just then that Paul joined us. "Paul, Richard is missing you need to search the entire house from top to bottom, and then the gardens, sheds, and garage, he must be here somewhere." I'm going to make Mr. and Mrs. Johnson a nice cup of hot tea. "Tea, tea, you think I'm going to drink tea, what I'm going to do, is call the police, that's what I'm going to do." "Yes, yes ok, you can call the police but the first thing they will ask you is, have you made a search of the house and garden. Just wait five minutes till Paul comes back, ok." "Ok five minutes, then I call the police." When Paul did return he had found nothing, no sign of Richard at all. Of course if anyone had looked at the painting in the entrance hall they would have seen a twelve year old boy sitting in the crowd on an old wooden bench, waving back at them. Betty Johnson was now on the phone to the police. They told her they would send a pc around as soon as possible.

Two hours later found Tony and Betty pacing around the house. I had sent Paul out searching the nearby streets and roads. Betty was just about to ask for the tenth time, "Where the hell are the police," when the door bell sounded. I opened the front door to find two policemen, standing there. One was a proper baby face, who did not look old enough to smoke or drink, the other was a proper wrinkled face, who looked too old, to smoke and drink. "Hello Mrs. Johnson?" asked baby face. "No I'm Mrs. Anderson the owner, Mrs. Johnson is waiting for you in the lounge."

"So let's get this straight," said wrinkle face, "you put Richard to bed in your room soon after you arrived here last night. You heard nothing in the night, and when you woke up this morning, Richard was gone." "Yep, that's what happened," Tony confirmed. So after they had written down all their notes, had a good look around the house and garden, they went back to the police station to file a missing persons report. When Paul and I were alone he could not hide the worried expression he wore on his face. "Judy we don't need this, what if they never find the boy, the place will be crawling with newspaper reporters it will be bad publicity. No one will ever want to come and stay here ever again, we could go bust." "Lets not panic yet," I told him, "chances are he will turn up, safe and sound." "But what if someone broke in last night and kidnapped him." "Paul no one broke in, he has not been kidnapped, wherever he is, he has not been kidnapped."

Days went by, Richard was still missing, the police went on local radio, and TV, adverts were put in newspapers, all to no avail. Not one lead did they have, even after the sniff dogs, had come and gone, and that's not to mention forensics going over everywhere with a fine tooth comb.

CHAPTER THREE

Doris was a fifty something, self confessed psychic and clairvoyant. It was true to say she had powers, always had, from as far back as she could remember. Her first memory was a painful one. She had been perhaps about twelve years old, and it happened one day at school. Doris was walking in a line filing out of a classroom, when her blond haired, math's teacher, had just rested her hand on to the shoulder of Doris. Doris froze, the pain that exploded in her vagina, was excruciating, nearly unbearable, well to a twelve old, anyway, and so was the image that appeared in her mind. An image that should never ever appear in the mind of a twelve year old girl. Her math's teacher Miss Wentworth was lying on her back, on her bed, with her legs wide open. Her boyfriend was kneeling in between them. In his hand he was holding a large, yellow ten inch banana. He now positioned one end of the banana in line to the entrance of the vagina belonging to Miss Wentworth. Slowly but firmly he was pushing it into her, and this was the pain poor Doris was feeling. "Doris, Doris are you alright?" Miss Wentworth was concerned, Doris was bending over in pain, "Quickly someone get me a chair for Doris." Miss Wentworth cried out. As soon as Doris was seated on the chair and Miss Wentworth had taken her hands off her, the pain and the image vanished, from her mind and her body.

However that was some forty odd years ago, now Doris was watching the media with interest, in particular the case of the twelve year old missing boy, Richard. She just had a strange feeling coming from where she didn't know, but a feeling never the less, a strong feeling that she could help. And it was that feeling that led her down to the police station that very afternoon. She walked up to the front desk and informed the policewoman on duty that she wanted to talk to someone about the missing boy. "I'm sorry" the policewoman informed her, "There is no one available to see you at the moment. Do you have any information, or have you seen him somewhere." "Well no I don't, and no I haven't seen him, but I'm sure I can help." "And just how can you help madam?" "I can, tell you that, you see I'm a psychic, I can feel and sense things, which you can't." "Yes madam of course you can, now please move on there is a queue forming behind you." But Doris was not going to be put off that easily, she quickly reached out her hand and laid it on top of the policewoman's hand which was resting on top of the desk. "Madam remove your hand now," Doris held it there just for a moment longer. "Yes I will remove my hand and I can also tell you that at the age of sixteen you lost your virginity in a bus shelter, to your boyfriend at the time, who you called Blue." The policewoman looked at

Doris with her mouth agape. "How could you possibly know-" she started to say, and then stopped. Ok, then madam please take a seat over there and someone will be with you shortly.

And less than twenty minutes later, found Doris Evens and detective John Davis, inside interview room one. John was not happy not happy at all, he felt he was in a no win situation. If indeed this psychic woman could help find the boy, then the public would say "What did a psychic do that the police couldn't." Or on the other hand if she didn't find the boy, the public would say "why does our police department have to rely on psychic mumbo jumbo." "Ok, ok," said John at last, "we will give it a try, but just as long as you understand anything you might find out, is top secret, and you must not talk to anyone about it, is that understood?" "Yes sir loud and clear." Doris assured him.

CHAPTER FOUR

Poor Richard was not a happy twelve year old, or rather he had been. He had been until his fairy Godmother had come to him in the night, and taken him away from his warm bed, and his mum and dad. His new fairy Godmother had told him she would show him her house, show him where she lived, and would then take him home again. It's true she did show Richard her house, and where she lived, however when it came to take him home again. She asked him "Don't you like it here Richard?" To which Richard replied, "I want my mum and dad, and I don't like the smell here." His fairy Godmother then asked him "do you know what that smell is Richard?" "Well no I don't," Richard told her. "That smell is of old rotting dead bodies coming up from the earth, dead, bodies that have been half eaten away by worms and slugs and rats and all things nice." "No fairy Godmother, those things aren't nice at all." Richard protested. "Oh dear Richard, that's what you think is it? Well your fairy Godmother is going to have to teach you a lesson, you bad, bad, ungrateful boy."

Without further ado she grabbed Richard's hand, tight, so tight it made Richard cry out in shock and pain. She then dragged him into her dirty wooden bad smelling kitchen. In the centre standing over an as yet unlit fire was a very large empty cooking pot. Empty that is until she bent over picked up and lifted Richard into the air with ease, and dropped him into the cooking pot. Richard was now sobbing and pleading to be let out. The cooking pot was so large, poor Richard could only just see over the top rim, even standing on tiptoe. "Please, please let me go I'll be good really I will." Pleaded Richard. "Not yet Richard my dear, not until you have learnt your lesson." said his fairy Godmother, who then lifted down a thick black dusty old book, from her dirty wooden shelf. She placed it on the dirty dusty table and leafed through the worn yellow pages. At last she found the page she was looking for. She then started talking with words Richard had never heard of before. Before long Richard sensed a stirring a movement in the bottom of the cooking pot. He looked down at his feet. Immediately Richard started running on the spot, the entire bottom of the cooking pot was now filled with rats, mice, worms, slugs, all trying to engulf a now petrified, screaming shouting and sobbing Richard. The rats and mice were the quickest, in no time at all they were running up his legs, biting, scratching, at his raw legs. Now they covered his tummy, his chest, his shoulders his face his head. His arms and hand were flying about in panic, trying to dislodge them from his body. But as soon as he dislodged one or two they were quickly replaced by three more, which were all waiting in turn to take a bit of his tender skin and flesh. When his fairy Godmother had decided he had had enough, she reached into the cooking pot grabbed hold of both his hands, firmly and pulled him out of the pot. As soon as she pulled him from the pot all the rats, mice, worms, and slugs disappeared as quick as they had come. As soon as she let him go, he ran, he ran as fast as he could, out of the kitchen, out the back door, down the dirty dusty cobbled streets. Every now and then he would look over his shoulder, to see if she was chasing after him or not. When at last he was certain she was not chasing after him he slowed his pace, and started to wonder where he was going to find a hiding place. Where would he be safe? But more importantly how was he going to get back home, to his mum and dad. He now started to walk back to the market square, still looking back over his shoulder every now and then. When he arrived back at the market square, he was surprised to see his fairy Godmother back up on the hanging stage with the metal chain once more around her neck, just like before. The painter was still there also still with the same brush in hand. He sat down on the dirty dusty ground underneath the wooden bench, just in case his fairy Godmother happened to look in his direction.

The very next day bright and early found D.I Davis and Doris, ringing the door bell belonging to Judy and Paul's guest house. "Thank you both for coming, Paul told them as he stood back from the door to allow them easy access into the house. Doris however took three steps into the entrance hall, before she stood stock still. Her thumb and four finger of her right hand was busy holding her nose. "Oh my God," exclaimed

"Doris whatever is that smell?" I had just joined the group with Betty, we all sniffed, long and hard but not one of us could smell anything. Doris looked around and when she saw the painting, she took a small step backwards. "Where did you get that painting? How long have you had it?" She wanted to know. Betty was now looking at the painting long and hard, Before Paul could answer Doris's question, Betty pointed at the picture, and shouted out. "LOOK, there he is under the seat, its Richard, Richard is in the painting, we've found him look, he is in the picture. Tony didn't even look at the painting; instead he rested his right hand on Betty's shoulder. "Now come on Betty that's not possible and you know it." Tony looked at Doris and the D.I "I'm sorry" he said my wife has been under a lot of pressure these last few days and-" "Tony I am not seeing things," Betty interrupted, "there look for yourself, It's Richard I know it is." "Paul I told you not to hang up that painting didn't I?" I said. Now Tony was getting on his high horse, he moved forward reaching up for the painting. "Well I'll get rid of the painting, I'll damn well burn it." "NO" shouted Doris "you must not do that, if that is Richard in the painting, and I'm not saying it is, but if it is, and you burn the painting, Richard will be lost to us for eternity, and not just lost to us, his immortal soul will also be lost to-" "Will you all just shut up," Tony interrupted, "just listen to your yourselves, who in their right minds would be talking about a boy, a real boy trapped inside a old painting." I held up both my hand, "wow, wow, wow," I said, lets all calm down, we will all go into the lounge with a nice pot of tea and talk about this, ok?" "Well I don't know about anyone else but I need something a hell of a lot stronger than tea." D.I Davis told everyone.

At last we were all seated in the lounge, all drinking tea, well that is except the D.I who was more than happy with a large brandy, and, who wouldn't be? The D.I turned to Doris, "So Doris is it possible, is it possible that Richard is in the painting?" "If you could smell, what I can smell, the smell coming from that painting is,.....lets say unholy, unnatural, the painting is a window, if you like, a window to the past, or a window from the past to the present, even a doorway, a doorway to the past, or from the past to the present." Poor Tony just sat in the arm chair shaking his head from side to side. Betty on the other hand was ready to believe in whatever Doris had to say. "So" Doris I asked, "Why does not Richard just come back, out of the painting?" "Because most of the time the window or door is closed." Now Paul was getting into the sprite of things, because he asked "Doris can you, can you open the painting, or the door leading to.......well leading to the past?" "I'm not sure, I've never tried to do anything like that before, but it can be dangerous, while the painting is open connecting the past and present, connecting the good and the evil, anything will be able to past through it. And we will be powerless to stop it. Richard did not open the painting on his own, someone or something opened it, and while it was open, just took Richard through it." Now it was the turn of the D.I to speak, "So if we can open the painting Richard could just come back, to us?" "Well in theory yes." "This calls for a vote, a show of hands," I told everyone, "everyone in favour of Doris trying to open the painting raise your hand."

Eventually the only hand not raised belonged to Tony. We all then made our way back into the hall way, and all of us stopped and just looked at the painting. "Oh my God" exclaimed Betty, look, he's gone, look, he's no longer under the wooden bench, where's he gone, Doris? Has he come back here?" "No he is still in that time frame, he has just gone out of view of the painting that's all, remember beyond that painting, everything is the same as it was three hundred years ago." "So" I said "do we just wait and see if he comes back into view of the painting, or.......or do we go into the painting to try to find him?" "Yes, yes we go into the painting and try to find him." said Richard's mother. "You can't go alone," I told her, "I'm going with you. Paul and Tony then tried ganging up on D.I Davis. "You have to stop them, you can't let them go into, into God alone knows what or where." "No power on earth will stop a mother from doing everything in her power to find her lost child. Even if it does mean going into a painting." My right hand reached up and closed around my gold cross, which I had not taken off since it was given to me by a stranger at my front door, way back when we lived in Olton Boards. Back then it had saved my life. Paul also had one, which he did, foolishly take off and he paid for that mistake, by losing his soul. But that is another story. "Paul give Betty your cross, we don't know what we are going to be up against in that painting." "But remember," said Doris, the danger may not just come from just a evil element, you could be in more danger from the human element as well. The cross will only protect you from all things evil; it will not protect you from the 1700's humans." Poor Tony was having a bad time, "Any moment now and I'm going to wake up in a mental hospital, I just know I am," he said. Betty was becoming inpatient, "come on Doris try and open the painting, we are ready to go."

"And just whom is ye a hiding from, me lad under this here seating." Richard had thought he was safe here; his fairy Godmother was up on the hanging stage again, with the metal chain around her neck. Which is why Richard thought he was safe? He looked up at the sound of the deep female voice. In ten years time Richard would call it a sexy, deep, female voice. He looked up into the dirty face of a woman about the same age of his own mother. He took a quick look into her bright blue eyes. Her blond hair gently blowing in the breeze. "Yes ye, I be talking to ye, what be, ye title ye go by?" "I'm sorry I don't understand." Stammered Richard. "She mean, what name do ye go by, joined in the painter, to Richard's right." "It's Richard," he mumbled. "My title be Ruby," she told him, as she gave him a nice smile. Or, it would have been a nice smile if she had more than four teeth in her mouth. "Ye look like ye need a good grub up." "Sorry I don't know what you mean." apologized Richard, for the second time. "Grub up, eat, food, do ye know what that do mean?" "Yes I am hungry," "then get ye out to here, and we go yonder. Just where might ye be coming from, to talk the such as ye talk, and the way ye dress, such as the like, I before never seen." Richard had by now come out of his hiding place and was now standing before Ruby. "I think," started Richard "these are the olden days, and I come from the new days. "Never ye mind about all this now, how old ye be?" "I'm twelve" "that be good, you look a good strong strapping lad, you serve me well good, and I feed you well good, now let us be gone." Richard did not really know what Ruby was talking about, but he did understood she would feed him, and he was hungry. He therefore let her lead him by the hand through the dirty cobbled streets. For the first time he was now feeling out of place when he saw the kind of clothes everyone else were wearing. Now Ruby was leading him down a narrow cobbled street with shops on either side, on the left was a bakers, he saw a woman squatted down over the gutter on the edge of the street with her skirt pulled up round her waist. At first Richard did not realize what she was doing. "What's that woman doing," asked Richard, "She be just relieving herself." Ruby answered. And sure enough he saw a yellow puddle gathering in the gutter beneath her. This then partly explained, to Richard the bad smell, it was of stale urine. The only time when the streets and gutters were cleaned was when it rained. Ruby tugged his arm, come, hurry we be here now. Ruby pulled him into a wooden building, the hanging sign outside said, Ale House. "This be your new workhouse, you belong to me from as now." "But I want to go home, I want my mum," Richard protested. "I be your Mum as of now, Ruby told him. She dragged him across the sawdust covered wooden floor. "Look, look, Albert, look ye what I have here." The Albert she was addressing was a bold fat dirty looking man behind the bar." "What ye be doing with that young brat?" Albert wanted to know. "He be our new barrel boy here to serve us our every need." Ruby told him. "Ye come here by me and I will show ye your first job." Ruby gave another hard tug on Richard's arm. She dragged him behind the bar and showed him six empty wooden beer barrels stacked up all along the floor under the bar. "Now ye watch and ye do learn, as Richard watched Ruby took hold of one barrel and tipped it onto it's side. She then steered it in the direction of the open door leading out into the yard. Next she stood behind it and rolled it over and over along the floor. She rolled it right out the door, out into the yard and then towards a pile of about ten or more also empty barrels. "This here heap is empty barrels, bring out one and take inside, a full up one from this here heap from over yonder." When Richard didn't move, she took careful aim with her right booted foot and kicked him hard on his bum. This sent Richard down onto his knees. Ruby reached down grabbed Richard's left ear and pulled him back up onto his feet. Richard was fighting back the tears. With big tears rolling down his cheeks Ruby dragged him by his ear across the yard and over to the pile of full beer barrels. "Now ye do like I did do," she demanded. Richard took hold of the top of the barrel, it was heavier than he had expected. With a struggle he managed to tip it over onto its side. It took all his might to roll it across the yard and into the Ale house. Once inside Albert was ready to take it from him, and stack it where he wanted it. Albert rebuked Ruby, "Ye go easy on the young brat, will ye the beer barrel is nearly as big as the brat be himself."

Again that night when Richard was seated at the table with Ruby eating some bread and gruel, he asked to go home. "Not till Ye have finished ye work and paid for ye grub." was her reply. It was after supper Ruby had another job for Richard. Hanging on the kitchen wall was a half tin bath, which Ruby took down and rested it on the wooden kitchen floor. The fire which was ablaze in the cast iron oven was heating up large pots of water. "Right" Ruby told Richard, It be ye job to bath me, empty the pots of that there warm water into the bath now, while I take off me garments." Without argument and without understanding what was required of him Richard quickly emptied the pots of warm water into the tin bath. What a shock poor Richard got when he looked up at Ruby. She was standing there without a stitch of clothing on her body. Now Richard had never seen a naked woman before, not even in a picture. And not even his own mother, in real life, and now here he was standing less than ten feet away from a naked Ruby. Even although he was only twelve, well nearly thirteen really, Richard was fascinated, he could not tear his eyes away. Ruby's ample, naked breasts with rose bud nipples were just the right shape and size for any male of any age. His glaze travelled slowly down from her breast's to her flat stomach, then down further still, her legs, he noticed were slightly parted. "Will ye stop staring at thee, have ye not ever seen a clothes less woman before now." "No, never," Richard responded. A smile appeared on her lips. "Well I never did, then ye will be wanting to be giving thee a wash all over then." With that Ruby walked over to the bath stepped in and sat her self down into the warm water. She then treated Richard to her special smile. "Come, come over to here," Ruby said, "here now pick up my wash rag, rub on some coal soap, and wash all over my neck. Not too quickly, now, slowly, slowly does it, you are so good at washing, Richard, yes ye are. Now my arms, all the way to my hands, yes now all the way back up, and underneath." Richard was experiencing a new emotion; he had never before seen a naked woman let alone wash one. "Now slowly real slow," prompted Ruby "wash my breasts." Richard did just that, he dipped the wash rag into the water, and then gently and slowly rubbed it all over Ruby's ample breasts. He felt the unevenness as the wash rag pasted over her now erect nipples. Ruby let out a low moan, from deep down in her throat, "oh that feels so really well good. Now move down lower, wash over my tummy, yes lower, lower." Ruby then lifted her left leg out of the bath. "Thee foot Richard, wash thee foot, oh yes now up higher, yes my knee, keep coming up to thee thigh yes, inside thee thigh up further, oh yes, oh yes. Now wash in between thee legs, wash my vagina, gently, yes backwards and forward, dare ye not to stop, oh ye must keep on going, oooohhhhh." Ruby now threw back her head she knew her orgasm was fast approaching, her whole body stiffened and arched she pressed her vagina tighter against Richard's hand, until her orgasm washed over her. "Oh, oh Richard, thank ye, thank ye, now pass me a drying cloth, she said as she stood herself up in the now nearly cold bath water. Richard passed her the drying cloth and Ruby started to dry off her arms and shoulders. Then her breasts. Suddenly she tightly crossed her legs, and slightly bent herself forward. "Oh quickly Richard pass to me the potty I must quickly relieve myself, oh quickly." Richard picked up the potty and walked over to Ruby, and held it out to her. "Ye hold it for thee," as she said that she opened her legs, Richard could see was urinating already because it was running down the inside of her legs. But he pushed the potty forward in between her legs and most of it splashed into the potty. The disruptive and rowdy noise coming from the bar was now at its peak. Albert was serving in there all alone, now his gruff voice was calling for Ruby and Richard to go and help him. All Richard wanted to was go to bed, but before that he had another three hours work ahead of him.

The very next day at breakfast he was seated at the table with Albert and Ruby. He again asked if he could go home. Albert lost his tempter he arose from his chair, reached over and gave Richard a hard back hander right across his face. "Why, why ye ungrateful spoilt brat, we give ye grub, work, and a bed, and then ye wanting to go home. Richard did not want Ruby to see him cry again, but he could not hold back the tears. He had only been here for a day and he was exhausted already. Today was going to be worst for Richard. His first job of the day was to carry a large wicker basket across to the bakers, and bring back today's bread. Next it was down to the butchers for tripe, and sausages. Then he had to wash all Ruby's and Albert's clothes, then it was back to barrel rolling. Remembering the back hander he had at breakfast he did not dare to ask to go home again.

CHAPTER FIVE

Doris was standing before the painting with the palms of her hands facing it, with her eyes shut tight. Just when everyone was thinking nothing was going to happen, Tony let out a groan. The reason for this was the painting was expanding; it was growing larger and larger. Until at last, just like before the whole wall had turned into the painting. "Go quickly, quick go, I don't know how long I can hold it open for." Doris told us. I looked at Betty, Betty looked at me, and we knew it was now or never, so we held hands and both of us stepped into the wall, into the painting. We had also both just stepped into the 1700's. We looked around, at the market square, we saw the woman who was about to be hanged, the crowd, watching and waiting, the artist with his easel and paints. And the smell was overwhelming. We had only been standing there for a couple of minutes but already we were getting strange looks, from people. "Its our clothes," I said to Betty, "I was going to say lets split up, we would double our chances of finding him, but on second thoughts maybe we should stick together." "Yes I think you're right about that." Betty answered. "I'm trying to put myself into Richards's shoes," I told Betty, "which way would he go do you think." "Maybe towards the shops," Betty replied, "but the fact he has no money to buy anything, anyway, so I just don't know." "Well we have to start somewhere, so it might as well be the shops." I told Betty. So we both set off in the general direction of the shops. We left the market square behind, and turned down a narrow dirty cobbled street, as it happened both me and Betty were wearing jeans, and going by all the looks we were getting no one here had of course never seen jeans before. We passed butchers, bakers, a candle stick makers and an ale house. I was so busy looking at all the old wooden shops I very nearly bumped into a man in a long black cape standing over the gutter urinating, and proudly showing everyone his six inch limp penis at the same time. Betty and I could not help ourselves and burst into fits of giggles as we walked past. "Joking apart," Betty told me, "I will need to find a ladies loo myself, pretty soon." "Judging by that I'm not too sure if they have such things as loo's here," I said. After about two hours, we must have searched all the streets around about, and no sign of Richard what-so-ever. By now we were hot, thirsty, and we had still not found any loos. "So what do we do now?" Asked Betty, we have no money to buy food or drink and I'm getting desperate for a pee." "We have to go back to the painting and try to get back through it, get back home, and then come up with a plan, a plan of action, after all we have been here once we will be able to come back another time." Betty did not like the idea of going back without

Richard, but as she had no better suggestion, and as she kept crossing and uncrossing her legs, she agreed. So we started the walk back to the market square. The square was now a hive of activity people were rushing about to and fro setting up wooden market stalls, to sell all kinds of ware's. We had only just started the walk across the square when we heard a commotion behind us. We turned to see a cart drawn by two horses, and running along side the cart were about twelve soldiers, well they looked like solders anyway, because they all carried long swords, on their belts. The horse and cart stopped just behind us, we then found ourselves surrounded by the soldiers. "STOP YE IN THE NAME OF THE KING." Shouted the nearest soldier. My history was not that good so which king he was talking about I didn't know. "In the name of the king state ye your business here," "We are looking for a lost small boy, have you seen him by any chance." I asked. "Where ye be from attired as ye both be," "we are from Hastings," I told them. "Ye lie, that attire is not coming from Hastings, now in the name of the king I ask ye once more, where are ye from?" "We really are from Hastings," I repeated, "just not from this time, from this year." "Then what year is ye both coming from?" "From the year 2007." I said. Betty was saying nothing she was too busy hopping from one foot to another. "Then in the name of the king I arrest ye both, for the crime of witch craft, for it be only a witch who can travel in and out of the years. Now hold out ye hands in front of ye." Now betty did speak up, no you don't understand, we are not witches we are just looking for my son." the nearest soldier half turned away from her, before spinning back around quickly and giving her a hard back hander right across her face. Betty let out a scream, before staggered backwards right into the open arms of another soldier, who then placed his arms right across Betty's chest. He held her there in his vice like grip. Another soldier took hold of both her hands and pulled them out in front of her. While another one shackled both hands together using a rusty pair of metal handcuffs. The soldier still held Betty close to him he could feel the pressure of her backside pressing into his groin, holding her in place he started walking towards the back of the cart. "Now, get ye aboard the cart," he ordered, and released her from his embrace, but not before he placed both his hands over each of her breast's, and gently squeezed. When I saw what they did to Betty, I held out both my hand which were then also handcuffed. They ordered me up onto the cart, and I sat down next to Betty. "Are you ok?" I asked her "your face looks well red." "It's not my face I'm worried about," she confided, it's my jeans I'm worried about, because, oh, I'm nearly wetting myself. I don't know how much longer I can hang on. The cart trundled through the cobbled streets I did feel sorry for Betty for every bump, brought a pained expression to her face. Soon we could see up ahead the king's castle. The big heavy double wooden doors were slowly opened as we approached. Once inside, the cart crossed the near empty court yard and stopped outside the entrance door leading to the cells in the dungeon. The soldier who had groped Betty's breast's, roughly grabbed hold of her by her left arm and pulled her to her feet, "this way ye sullied slut." he told her. "And ye move yourself also," another soldier said to me. We were led down a darkened corridor poor Betty was bending at the waist as she hobbled along. On either side of the corridor were cells with iron bar gates. When we came to the first empty cell the soldier holding on the Betty's arm pushed her inside and followed her in. He turned to another soldier and told him to lock the iron bar gate. Which he did, he then turn to face Betty who was standing bobbing up and down with legs tightly crossed. "Please" said Betty I need the toilet badly," "Ha ha ha," laughed the soldier, ye just be a saying that so that I do not be a wanting to rape ye." "Oh no please I really do need to go bad," with that the soldier stepped up closer to Betty took hold of her shoulders and spun her around so her back was facing him. He then put both arms around her middle and fumbled for the button of her jeans. It came undone at his first attempt, the zip however proved more of a problem for him. The more he tried to undo it the more Betty wiggled, and the more she wiggled, the more her backside pressed up hard against the crotch of the soldier. Betty was now starting to feel his growing erection. Betty started to whimper, "No please, please leave me alone." she begged. This however fell on deaf ears, at last he got Betty's zipper undone, and using both hands he peeled down her jeans and panties till they were around her ankles. The soldier then freed his nine inch erect penis; he then gripped the back of her neck with his left hand and pushed it forward. "Now bend ye over," he commanded, Betty's legs were still tightly crossed. Now she could feel his penis trying to push its way in, searching for her vagina. "No please, please don't, please. "Open ye legs ye slut," he demanded,

Betty didn't want to; she knew if she did she would lose control of her bladder completely. The soldier now reached up with his right hand grabbed a hand full of Betty's hair and tugged hard. The shock made Betty cry out, it also made her relax her bladder for a second. A warm, short spurt squirted from her vagina. Now Betty just wanted this to be over, slowly she slightly parted her legs, as soon as she did so his penis was there, pushing at the entrance to her vagina. She felt another warm spurt squirt from her aching vagina. Then with one hard push from the soldier his penis rammed its way in, all nine inches of it right up to the hilt. That was it Betty could hold on not another second, she relaxed her muscles, and the flood gates opened.

The trial of Betty and I took place in the assizes before the king. Sorry did I say trial? Its was not a trial owning to the fact we had no opportunity to defend ourselves. Just as poor Betty could not defend herself from the brutal rape she had to endure. We were both found guilty of witch craft; our sentence was to be death, from hanging.

At least our cells were next to each other so we could talk that night. "So, and just how do you propose to get us both out of this bloody muddle, tomorrow we will both be hanged, and its all your fault," Betty said. I had no argument to give because she was right it was my entire fault, or rather Paul's fault for bringing home that painting and then hanging it up. Now the soldiers were going round making sure all the iron bar cell gates were all locked for the night. They were not on duty all night, which meant that was our only chance of escape. "Oh yes very cleaver Judy" Betty said, "and how do you purpose to unlock the gates? You just tell me that." Betty was right even with all the soldiers gone for the night we were going nowhere. It was then the gold cross around my neck started to grow warm. Yes of course, I then remembered the boat 'Pretty Emmylou' it had been called, and the locked toilet door, and how I opened it with the hot gold cross. I whispered to Betty wait till all the soldiers have gone then I have a plan," I think we may have waited about an hour after they had gone. I couldn't be sure because since we had been here our watches had both stopped. I got up and walked to the locked gate, reached up and took hold of the cross, lent forward and pressed the gold cross against the iron gate lock. Sure enough with aloud click and the lock opened. I slowly opened the gate looked up and down the corridor saw no one, and shutting the gate behind me, rushed to Betty's cell and did the same thing. "How the hell did you do that?" Betty wanted to know. "Later, later, I told her lets get going for now. We rushed up the corridor till we came to the door leading to the court yard. I unlocked this one in the same way; we then walked all around the outside of the court yard till we came to the main entrance double doors. Again this one we opened in the same way, we passed through it and we were now free of the castle. We now had a long walk back to the market square. We walked along the edge of the road ready to dart into the tree's for cover should we encounter any of the kings soldiers. However as it was night time our escape would not be detected until the morning.

Richard also had a plan, a plan to escape from Ruby and Albert; it did mean waiting till early morning when they were still both asleep, in bed. If of course he could wake himself up in time.

The next day it was the sound of the cock crowing that woke Richard, being as quick as he could he got dressed, the old clothes that Ruby had found for him were much better than his pajamas, for walking the streets. Even although they were too large for him. Richard then crept down the stairs, across the bar and slowly withdrew the large iron bolts which locked the double wooden doors. Its was still fairly dark outside, and Richard didn't like the dark, never had done. But he told himself it was now or never. He knew he had to find his way back to the market square; it was after all the painting which had brought him here in the first place. That and his fairy Godmother, if in fact she was his fairy Godmother. He told himself he was too old to believe in fairies or fairy Godmothers, come to that. Being as quiet as he could he closed the bar door behind him and rushed along the urine smelling cobbled street. Even after all this time he had still not got use to that smell. When he arrived at the square it was just the same as when he had left it with Ruby, all those days ago. It was now starting to get really light, which pleased Richard, no end.

CHAPTER SIX

D.I Davis was now sitting in the Dog & Duck Public House, as it was now holiday season it was very busy even for a lunch time. He was starting to have preliminary serious uncertainties about his sanity, and who could blame him. For just a couple of hours age he had witnessed a old painting, turning into an entire wall, or was it the entire wall turning into a old painting. Either way, it made no difference, whichever way you looked at it. And if that was not enough, two commonplace, two ordinary, living women, then stepped into the wall, no, stepped into the painting, and had just, well, had just disappeared. Just maybe he thought to himself, another drink would help him come to terms with today's events. He picked up his empty glass from the table he was seated at, and made a beeline line for the bar. He had lost count of how many drinks he had, had, it made no difference, he told himself, how could he go to work this afternoon while he was hallucinating? It was the only explanation. At least the barmaid behind the bar was not a hallucination. The D.I guessed she was maybe twenty, twenty one or twenty two at the most. She was wearing a white, tight, low cut tee shirt with no bra underneath, at her age she didn't need one anyway. She also wore a short black mini skirt, because the D.I thought to himself it would be a crime to hide those long, tanned, sexy legs. "Yes sir, same again is it?" She asked. She also had the brightest blue eyes the D.I had ever seen in his life. And her smile, she had protruding front teeth, which her dentist wanted to fit braces to. But to the D.I her teeth set in her face was the prettiest and sexiest combination he had ever uncounted in his entire life. "Yes sir, same again is it?" she asked again. D.I Davis then asked her "Oh my God, are you real or are you a hallucination?" "I have been called a lot of things before, but never a hallucination" she told him. "Well in that case yes please I will have the same again, and this time make it a double, please." "So does that mean it's a double, double, because the last one you had was a double." It was just then his mobile started playing "I can tell by your eyes, you must, have been crying for ever, and the stars, in your eyes don't mean nothing, their only a mirror," by Rod Steward. The D.I located his phone flicked it open and held it to his ear. "Hello D.I Davis? Its Paul here, Paul Andrews, just to let you know Richard, the boy has reappeared in the painting, as yet there is no sign of Judy or Betty. Doris is going to try to open the painting again to see if we can get him back. Just thought I would let you know." D.I Davis took the phone away from his ear and just looked at it. He did not know if that call was real or if it was part of the hallucinations that he thought he had been having. "Did you hear that?" he asked bright eyes. Still looking at his phone. "Well I did hear Rod Steward; I want that ring tone, where did you get it from?" Replied the mini skirted, tight tee shirted, sexy, young barmaid. So that then, now meant that his phone had actually rung, which meant the call was not a hallucination it really did happen. It really did ring. "Forget the drink, I'm off," slurred the D.I. "And the sex you wanted, assumed bright eyes, should I forget that as well?" with a wave of his hand, he walked away from the bar, he knew he was far too drunk to drive, but told himself it was only round the corner, and he would be careful.

Doris, Tony and Paul were excited; they could now see Richard was back in view, he was back in the painting. But they were all disappointed to see there was no sign of Betty or Judy. "Where can they be?" Paul asked no one in particular.

In fact Betty and I were exhausted we had been walking half the night, but now we were about to enter the market square from the opposite end from where Richard and the painting was located. Richard was looking at the painting, hoping for it to start getting bigger. Every now and again he would have a look around the square to make sure Albert or Ruby had not missed him and had come looking for him. Then as if in answer to a prayer as Richard looked at the back of the painting, it did start to grow bigger, and bigger. Now the back of the painting had gone, as Richard looked he could now see his dad, with the man they called Paul standing in the entrance hall, with a woman, who he had never seen before. Now Richard could see his dad gesturing to him, beckoning, to him to step forward, to step into the painting. "RICHARD, RICHARD, IS

THAT YOU?" Betty shouted Richard stopped and turned to see us running across the square towards him. When he realized it was his dear old mum, he started to run towards us, but he had only taken about six steps, before he froze in his tracks. The reason for this was, just entering the square behind us and chasing us, were six soldiers on horse back. Shouting at the top of his voice the lead soldier shouted "STOP YE BOTH IN THE NAME OF THE KING." Richard hesitated, not knowing what to do. Now he could hear his dad shouting "COME ON THIS WAY, RICHARD, INTO THE PAINTING NOW." Now Richard was shouting at the top of his voice. "QUICK MUM QUICK, INTO THE PAINTING." Now Betty and I were just ten feet away from Richard and the painting. The soldiers had brought their horses to a halt and were dismounting, to give chase on foot. The soldiers now drew their swords thinking that we had nowhere to go. However without further ado Betty, Richard and I jumped into the painting.

D.I Davis arrived outside of the guesthouse in his car without calamity. That is if you didn't count him mounting the pavement with his nearside front wheel. As he staggered down the front path leading to the front door, he saw the door standing ajar. He could also hear a lot of shouting, coming from inside. He opened the door and looked into the entrance hallway. First of all he saw Doris, and standing next to her shouting and gesturing wildly was Paul and Tony. Then, when he saw Betty, Richard and I, jump out from the hallway wall, and into the hallway he knew he must be hallucinating again, for sure. Once in the hall way, I led Betty and

Richard into the lounge and slammed the door shut. "QUICK, QUICK DORIS CLOSE THE PAINTING" Paul yelled. The D.I was now standing looking into the painting, trying to make out some kind of sense of it all. "LOOKOUT" shouted Tony; the D.I did not even realize that Tony was referring to him. For jumping right out of the painting and into the hallway with his sword held out in front of him was one of the kings soldiers. The soldier could not stop himself in time, did not even have time to lower his sword. The sharp blade penetrated the beer gut of D.I Davis, deeper and deeper it went in, until the sharp point of the blade, came out the other side and protruded from the back of D.I Davis. The soldier panicked he did not know where he was, he had stabbed a man with his sword, and now the sword was wedged in his guts. The kings Soldier turned on his heels and jumped back into the painting from whence he came. He only just made it, because then Doris managed to close the painting. By now the poor D.I had collapsed in a heap on the floor. "Anyone know first aid?" Paul asked, no one answered Tony and Doris were frozen by shock. Then lounge door opened slightly and I looked into the hall way. When I saw the wall was again a wall and I saw the D.I in a heap on the floor with a sword through him, I turned and said to, Betty and Richard. "Stay in here with the door shut ok?" I then went out into the hallway. The D.I was lying on his side, blood was pouring out from where the sword had penetrated his guts. It had also started to dribble from his mouth. "Well for Gods sake is no one going to call for an ambulance?" I asked. "Hold on lets not be too hasty here," Paul said. "Paul shut up, I said, I knew very well what Paul was thinking he could see the newspaper headline now, 'D.I MURDERED AT GUESTHOUSE' Paul did not want any bad publicity. Tony was now kneeling down by the side of the D.I "don't worry too much about the ambulance," he said, "because it won't do him any good. He just died." I turned walked down the hallway for the phone, to ring the police. "Judy, Judy, Judy," Paul said, lets not be too hasty, lets just take a while to think about this, shall we?" "Paul there is nothing to think about we have a murdered policeman in our hallway with sword from the 1700's stuck right through him." "Yes we do, and who murdered him that is what the police will want to know, they will be looking for someone to blame, and they won't care who, as long as they can arrest someone for murder. Who do you think it will be Judy? Me, you, Tony, Doris, Betty, Richard?" Now Doris spoke for the first time, "He's right, Paul's right; let's just take a while to think this through, shall we? They can't arrest a soldier from the year 1700, now can they, but they can arrest one of us, and they will, for as sure as, black is black, and white is white, they will, arrest one of us. If we all say it was a soldier from 1700 who murdered him, will they believe us, no of course they won't, and really who could blame them?" We could all see Doris was talking sense. Now Betty had opened the lounge door and was peeping out into the hallway. "What's going on," she asked. "Betty keep the door shut for five more minutes, I wanted to lay a sheet over our dead body, before Richard came out and saw it. When they did emerge from the lounge we told Betty about everything we had been talking about. "But what about the body, we will get found out, one way or another they will find us out." Betty was near to tears. "But not if they have no body, no body, no evidence, no crime." I reassured everyone. "And just what the hell do we do with the body; bury it in the fucking garden, or what?" Demanded a now very upset Betty. Tony moved over to Betty and put his right arm around her shoulder. It was Doris who came up with the answer. "No what we do is, I open the painting, one more time, we then simply throw the body into the painting, throw it into the year 1700. I then close it one last time; we then take down the painting take it out side and burn it, that's what we do." We were all thinking about this when our thoughts were interrupted by Rod Steward singing, "I can tell by your eyes, you must, have been crying for ever, and the stars, in your eyes don't mean nothing, their only a mirror." I think we all jumped, "What the hell is that," asked a jumpy Betty. "It's just a phone, a mobile ringing, that's all." I tried to reassure her. By now it had stopped ringing, but now our land line started ringing instead. I went to answer it. "Hello Mrs. Andrews it's the Hastings police station here, we are trying to locate D.I Davis is he with you by any chance?" "Err no sorry he was here but then he left, he did say he would be back later," I lied. After I replaced the receiver I wanted this over with, as I'm sure we all did. "Who was it?" Paul wanted to know. "No one it doesn't matter." I told him. "Now come on Doris lets get this dirty deed done shall we?" I asked. Everyone nodded their head in approval, and agreement.

CHAPTER SEVEN

However before Doris could start to open the painting it started to open by itself. "What the hell?" said Doris more to herself than to anyone else? Doris could not stop it from opening, how could she, it was not her who started it opening. As before the painting grew larger and larger, until as before it was the size of the wall. All we could do was to stand and stare. We then all jumped back in surprise, as we watched, witch Hickes jump out the painting and into our hallway. I stepped in front of Richard I don't know why I did, I just did. Doris held up both her hands and made a cross with her two index fingers. "You have no business here, now be you gone." Doris said with authority. "I be gone when you give me what be mine," said the witch. "And what might that be?" asked Doris. The witch pointed to behind me, "It be the brat of course, it be the brat, give me what I want and I will be gone, for good." "NO NEVER WE WILL NEVER GIVE UP THE BOY." I shouted. "So be it, we will see," said the witch. I then took hold of my gold cross around my neck and held it up facing the witch.

Doris then moved over to be by my side, still making a cross with her two index fingers. "Everyone get behind us," I said to Paul, Tony and Betty. It then started as a breeze, which grew in strength, I then realized it was not a breeze, no this was a suction, as if the painting had become a strong giant Hoover, it was trying to suck us all in into the painting. As the suction got stronger and louder so did the laugh of the witch. I could feel a frightened Richard hanging onto my waist for dear life. And it may well have been as well, his life that was at stake here. Now other pictures and painting that once hung on the walls were being sucked up, and went whishing over our heads. If it had not been for the power of the cross we would have been sucked in as well. The suction became so strong it was lifting the rugs and carpets up off the flooring; these also went flying past us. The sheet I had used to cover D.I Davis had long gone, had long been sucked up. Now his dead body was elevated above the floor, it was floating, hesitating, then with a whoosh it was gone also, it was sucked into the painting. When there was nothing left for the suction to suck up, apart from us, but the cross being more powerful than the Witch. We were going nowhere. Afterwards, after the suction had died down, not one of us could agree on where the witch had gone to. In the confusion Betty thought she had seen the witch being sucked into the painting itself. Paul said he thought she went floating out the front door. Tony did not have any opinion at all. And as for Doris she could not wait to burn the painting. Paul reached up and took down the painting off the wall. We then all followed him out into the backyard and garden. Paul placed the painting in the middle of the path. He went into the garage and came back with the petrol for the lawn mower, which he poured over the painting. Without another word from anyone he struck a match and dropped it onto the painting, which burst into flames.

CHAPTER EIGHT

All of this happened some ten years ago. Yes of course the police investigated the disappearance of D.I Davis. Because as far as the police were aware, that is what it was, a disappearance. As far as the police were aware the last person to see him alive and well, was a sexy, young barmaid who assumed, and assumed rightly that he wanted to have sex with her. The file belonging to the D.I was never closed. And as I said before, no body, no evidence, no crime. Our guesthouse was fully booked every year, and made us a comfortable living.

As for poor Doris She plucked up the courage to go to see her Doctor. She had discovered a lump in her left Breast. "I'm sure its nothing her Doctor reassured her, but we will have a mammogram done just to check it out. Just eight months later, Doris passed away.

And Richard, his adventure back into the 1700's just seemed like some distance dream. He had married into a rich family he had everything he had ever dreamed of, until that is one cold dark night, in June, yes in June. It had been the coldest June Richard could ever remember. He was in bed with his rich wife Linda, who, for about the third time that day was demanding sex. The TV was tuned into a news channel. Linda did like to listen to the news as she made love. The news story was covering the new arrival of the new prime minister to No.10 Downing Street. Not only the arrival of the prime minister but also his wife as well. "Oh my God" said Linda "just look at her Richard she is so ugly, I have never seen anyone as ugly as her before." Richard stopped in mid thrust, and turned his head so he could see the TV. The image of the ugly woman, Linda referred to, made him lose his erection instantly. Richard knew who she was even before the news reader told him. "And here we have a big smile, from whom; some people are already starting to call, the wicked witch of he west."

Written By:
John P. Smith
June 2009